HIS DANGEROUS DESIRE

BAD BOY BRATVA

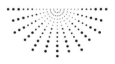

GIA BAILEY

BAD BOY BRATVA

My name is Karim Volkov, last year, I died.

It was a strange thing, living as a dead man. Existing in the places between awake and asleep, haunting the shadows of places I used to know. A twilight half-life, but I deserved nothing more. I didn't even deserve to rest my weary bones in the dirt, not while she was still locked in the hell of my making.

I had no earthly wants except her freedom. My sister. Elena. I had long ago given up hope of a life filled with anything other than blood and regret. I would have happily accepted my fate, as long as I freed her first. It was my only desire. That, and to rain vengeance down on the man who stole both our lives.

But then a chance meeting with a woman who makes me want to live again, a woman who makes me wish I was whole, casts doubt in my heart.

There is no place for vengeance and love in me, they

cannot exist together. I'm torn between the past and the future, and only one can win.

CHAPTER ONE

*K*arim

England really was the sweet-smelling land that people talked about. It was a small thing, but country air unpolluted by chemical factories, or fires, seemed like too great a luxury to imagine, for someone like me. Someone who had grown up in the smog and grime of Moscow.

My brother was getting married, in a country estate no less. I wasn't invited, but I could hardly blame him, after all.

He thought I was dead, as did everyone else in attendance at the fine event.

I stayed in the shadows of the woods outside the walls of the grand building. This was it, my chance to get to my sister. I didn't think Igor Orlov would be releasing her from her prison anytime soon after this. It was today, or never, and I couldn't allow it to be never. My soul wouldn't rest until she was freed, and I couldn't live as a half-man, spirit of vengeance any longer.

I heard the soft babble of conversation, as guards passed by the walls on patrol. Volkov men? I didn't know a single one, save Ivan, my brother's trusted second in command. I'd turned my back on my brother and his way of life long ago, ignorantly selling myself and my sister into something far worse. That was just one of the sins that I would be tormented for, when my torn soul finally made it down below. Another dark tally on a list that would turn a devil's stomach.

I flipped my knife in my hands, a small distraction to count down the time, and keep me sharp. I liked to imagine it sinking into Igor Orlov's neck. Igor, one of the only men who knew I was still alive. The one who had lied to everyone.

I had no weapon except myself and this knife. Traveling to England had meant leaving behind anything else I might have gotten hold of in Russia, like a gun. It had taken every single penny I could beg, borrow or steal to get a new passport identity, and a ticket to reach this green and sweet smelling land. I would have liked to make my stand in Russia, and long before now, but Igor's security had made that impossible. He was a watchful, paranoid bastard, and there was no way I could have reached Elena, in the impenetrable fortress he called a house. Her prison.

The only person that Igor was afraid of, was Max. My brother. A man who commanded respect and fear in equal measure. He'd brought Elena to the wedding because to miss it, would have been to raise Max's suspicions. Even estranged families will attend a wedding and funeral.

Music sounded from inside the huge home, drifting on a breath of clean air toward me. Max, my brother, getting married. It would have saddened me that I wasn't present if I still had a heart to move. My heart was a pitted, cracked thing, and it beat for only one reason now, and one reason alone. Save Elena and exact vengeance in the most brutal way.

I stood, dusting my ripped and dirtied jeans off. Even the leaves and dirt from this fair land looked clean and new next to me. I was under no illusions of how I looked. Perhaps Elena wouldn't even know me when I finally saw her face again. The young man who'd been her brother was long gone. Who I was now, I'm not sure, but I wasn't him. The young Karim had preached a life of ideals, of turning from violence, of living a proud, peaceful life. I might laugh at the hand that fate had dealt those misguided ideas. Maybe some men can dream of that kind of life, but Volkovs were born with violence and darkness in their blood, and there had never been an escape waiting for me. Fate had taught it to me cruelly and thoroughly. Now, dying with honor, coated in Igor Orlov's blood was the most I could hope from this short and thoroughly terrible life.

I approached the wall where I had already found a good place to scale it, and listened for sounds. After a while, I started my climb. I should have been weaker, given my way of life, existing in the shadows, penniless and starved, but anger drove me. Anger is a fuel that never tires nor runs out.

I climbed quickly and dropped to the manicured green of the manor house lawn. The building was so beautiful, I stared at it dumbly for a moment. That such a place might exist in the same world as I did was a sobering thing. It seemed everything found its level, sooner or later. The thought was humbling, as always.

I started across the endless, beautiful grass toward the corner of the house, where a small outbuilding appeared to be empty. It was locked with a padlock, but I quickly opened it with my knife and crept inside. Gardening supplies filled it. It would make a good place to bide my time, where I might observe guests coming and going.

If my life were a movie, like the ones they make in Hollywood, I would have entered the party in a new suit, with my long hair tied back, clean-shaven and suave. I would have swept in like a secret agent, and taken Orlov out somehow with a clean and effortless kill, and liberated my sister, and rejoined my brother all at once. But my life was as far from that as one could be. Instead, I had no plan, I had no weapons, except myself. But in reality, that is often the case. All I had was my hatred and my anger. Because of that fuel, I needed no disguise. I would throw myself in the path of any danger, and I didn't expect to walk away. That made me a bomb that even Igor Orlov wouldn't be able to escape.

So, I watched the mansion, and I waited.

This day, it would end.

Today would be my last. I inhaled that sweet-scented air, and savored it, while I still could.

CHAPTER TWO

ani

When I turned thirty, I adopted a simple rule when it came to weddings.

Always drive.

It was a simple, yet elegant way to make sure I didn't end up tits up in the cake or doing the walk of shame from some groomsman's hotel room the next morning. At the grand old age of thirty, I had already done my share of creeping out, shoes in hand, to last me a lifetime. Well, it had happened once, and that was enough, I'd found. The memory still made me cringe enough to help me stick to my rule.

At weddings, I always drove.

Maxim and Prudence's wedding was no exception, though, it was by far the most lavish event I'd ever had the opportunity of being invited to. Being a nurse at Holloway General in London, number one must-visit locations for stabbings and overdoses, I hardly had time for socializing at all, never mind being invited to the mafia wedding of the decade.

That's right, my best friend had just married into the Russian mafia. It should have been weirder than it was. In fact, the whole thing had been terribly civilized. If not for the men with machine guns wandering around here and there, I'd have forgotten all about it.

I suppose as a nurse, and generally upstanding citizen, I should frown upon the Volkov family, and their activities and I'm sure I would, if I'd known every single one of them. But generally, I didn't mind Max. I didn't think he was a monster. Maybe that made me just as bad, I don't know.

Another benefit of driving is it gave you an excuse to cut out early. Yep, that's right, I'm the thirty-year-old party pooper who likes to leave the party right after the cake's been cut. My days of nightclubs and sticky bars are long behind me. Nothing ever good happens there, well, I guess the bride and groom met in one, but that's another story. Being a spinster with no one to dance with at your best friend's wedding demands an early exit surely? Ok, maybe it was just me, but in a desperate attempt to stick to water, and out of any other desperate single's beds, I made my excuses just after midnight and went to collect my things at the coat check. Luckily tonight I didn't have far to go. I was only driving to my parent's empty house, twenty minutes at most. I wouldn't be able to manage much more, exhausted from a day of wedding activities, cake, and smiling for photos.

The manor house the wedding was being held in was lavish, but not more lavish than the manor estates my friends now lived in with their mobster husbands. All while I was still holding down the fort in a one-bedroom, top-floor flat in North London. Truthfully, I didn't need fancy things. Before university, I'd volunteered abroad in Africa, and helped build a school in a small community. The memories of those days were still the best of my life. I had always planned to go back, once I was a fully qualified nurse, but then I was stuck with expensive rent, and bills from studying to pay off. Now, I was getting older, and my friends were all settling down. I started to worry I'd miss the boat, if I didn't stay in London, and try and meet someone. Yeah, that was working really well so far. The last date I'd gone on had taken me to a vegan place, gotten terrible diarrhea, and texted me to bring him wet wipes to the bathroom.

I took my coat and slid it on over my glitzy dress. Outside, flaming torches lined the graveled drive, and men in suits stood all over, with headsets and serious expressions. They looked out of place against a backdrop that could otherwise be straight out of Bridgerton. I gave my ticket to the valet and waited. It shouldn't be hard to find. I was one of the only guests who had driven themselves and did not have a chauffeur-driven, bullet-proof limo.

A harshly whispered conversation caught my attention as I waited. I turned to see a couple of security guys talking and smoking by the side of the building. They didn't have the rigorous deadly look of Maxim's guards.

"I don't understand, what happened?" one of them asked, in an English accent. Ah, so even the Russian mafia outsourced jobs these days.

"Elena Volkov is missing – she's disappeared,"

"Here you go," A voice spoke just beside me, catching me as I was leaning right around a white marble column and eavesdropping shamelessly. I jumped and turned. My car sat before the steps.

"Oh, yes, erm, thanks," I said clumsily, digging in my purse for a tip. It wasn't really a British custom to tip, and sure enough, all I had in my purse was a pound coin. I pressed it into the man's hand and gave him the most elegant smile I could muster. "Thank you ever so much," I murmured demurely, stepping daintily down the stairs as though it was a first-class ride awaiting me and not my ten-year-old Kia.

Still, the mess inside was comforting in an odd way, as was the tape of Alanis Morrisette that had been stuck in there since the first week I bought the car.

I drove slowly out the estate, not wanting to accidentally get shot or something.

The lights of the manor house faded quickly into the real inky night of the English countryside. I turned my lights to full-beam, and put my glasses on. There was no need to look glam now, was there?

I wound slowly along, cursing the overgrown summer hedgerows. Alanis's Jagged Little Pill accompanied me. Elena Volkov was missing? Volkov??

Ahead a shape moved by the side of the road, just outside the pool of my headlights. I slowed more. In this part of Hertfordshire, it wasn't uncommon to have deer leaping out at you while you were driving. The shadow moved toward the car, and I slammed on the breaks, as I stared at it in shock. The sight drove all other thoughts out of my head.

It wasn't a deer.

It wasn't an animal at all.

It was a man.

A man who was making right for the passenger side door.

I reached out for the door lock, giving a cry of fear, but was too slow. The door opened, and the man leaped inside.

"Please – drive," he urged as I stared at him in horror. He was dressed in black, and I could hardly make out his face. He had a hood up, and he was big, despite his hunched posture. He was folded protectively over his middle, and alarm bells were screaming in my head at the sight. He looked dangerous, and he'd just gotten into my car in the middle of nowhere in the dead of night. I reached for my phone, sitting in the drink well between us, and he reached out and grabbed my wrist. He squeezed, careless strength so much harder than I could have imagined, and I dropped the phone.

"What are you doing? Get out of here!" I cried, pulling my wrist from his hand. The man's breathing was labored, and he smelled of metal and fear. An all too familiar smell, to someone in my line of work. I looked at the hand he had grabbed and saw his red smeared fingerprints.

Blood.

This man was bleeding, probably heavily, from somewhere.

"Please, I won't hurt you, please just drive," the man muttered. I stared at him, paralyzed with indecision. I could drive him to a hospital, but who says he wasn't waiting to attack me once we were further from the wedding venue. Or he could die right here, and I'd have done nothing to stop it. I cursed under my breath.

"If you don't drive right now, they'll find me, and kill me. They'll probably kill you too, just for seeing me," he said quietly. He turned to look at me then, and the small car light overhead shone down on golden skin, stretched tightly over high cheekbones and a square jaw. He had dark eyes, full of pain and mystery. He was beautiful.

"In a few more minutes, I'll be too weak to move. If you want to, dump my dead body out then, but please, drive right now," he urged me once more, this time, those intense dark eyes locked on me. I had to make a decision, and there was no way to know which was right before doing it. There was something in his voice though, a desperation in his tone that

9

tugged at my heart. I couldn't walk away from an injured person, I just couldn't. It went against every instinct I had. Making my decision, right or wrongly, I turned the key, pushed the gas, and sped into the night.

CHAPTER THREE

Karim

If life hadn't taught me well enough that my plans were worthless, today really brought it home. Elena was gone, escaping herself with the help of some unknown man. I worried for her at the same time as I was elated. I hoped that man was stronger than me, connected, armed. Better. Of course, if I'd been a better, cleverer man, maybe I'd have made off for another country by now or hiked up to Scotland to live in a croft and meet a nice village girl to settle down with and make a new life. Instead, I was ready to pitch myself against the might of the man who had ruined my life, and no doubt die in the process. That was the kind of mad bastard I'd ended up being.

Just when I'd verified that she was gone, however, I'd run into Orlov's men, and been shot at. Shot on sight was clearly the order that Igor had for me, and they hadn't hesitated to carry it out. Luckily, no guests or other security were meant to have guns at the wedding, and Max's forces had descended on them swiftly, as I'd dragged my bleeding body away into the shadows.

"Go faster, if they catch us, you'll be killed," I told the woman whose car I'd landed in. My voice was harsh and she flinched. I had no gentleness left in me.

"You said we'd both be killed," she accused, as though that was somehow comforting to her.

"They might still need me. I might merely be punished, you, on the other hand, will be killed. To be clear, all you need to do is drive faster. This car is pretty much worthless, but it can manage that," I told her. Impatiently.

"This car is not worthless! It's in better shape than you right now," she protested hotly, but she did speed up a little, so that was something.

"Very true, but it's a low bar," I panted, pushing down a wave of dizziness to try and turn to see out the back. It was really quite impressive how my little used English was holding up under the events of the evening. I guessed all the money Max had put into tutoring Elena and I wasn't wasted after all. I only hoped my sister was remembering enough to ease her escape.

My reluctant driver bit her lip, her eyes shifting to the rear-view mirror and back again. It felt important to make this stranger understand that her life was in danger above all, for why would she care about mine?

She leaned her body forward as though that would make the car faster.

"Do you want me to drive?" I asked her roughly. I wasn't sure I'd manage it, with the profuse bleeding and all, but anything had to be better than her turtle's pace.

"No! It's my car, and anyway, you're hurt," she said, glancing over me with an assessing look.

"I could drive better shot than you are,' I growled at her.

"You've been shot?" she exclaimed. "Where exactly?"

"If you don't drive faster, it's not going to matter," I muttered to her. I was feeling woozy. The beating I'd gotten on the way out, plus the gunshot, and then staggering through the countryside waiting for a car to come along was starting to make my head swim. I couldn't pass out now, and leave myself to the mercy of this stranger, who looked like she'd have rather I hadn't gotten in the car. I knew the feeling. After all my grand plans and noble thoughts of sacrificing myself to kill Igor, I'd been shot and run away, and now, struggled to live. Was I still afraid of dying, even now? No, I wasn't afraid. I just hadn't settled my debt yet. I couldn't die while Igor lived.

I slumped further forward in my seat.

"What's your name?" I asked, mostly to distract myself from passing out.

"It's Dani. I'm Dani," she said, and I heard her voice moving away, as though she was speeding down a long tunnel, leaving me behind.

"Do you think you could sew up a bullet wound?"

"I know I can drive you to a hospital,"

"No, no hospital, we'll both die, and I'm not ready yet," I forced out. I couldn't die, not today. It was too soon. "Can you just patch me up a little, and I'll go, as soon as we're somewhere safe," I muttered. "Can you do that?"

"I'm a nurse, of course, I can," she snapped at me. I let out a laugh at that information. After all this time, a lucky break? It seemed impossible for a man like me. Darkness swallowed me whole.

ani

So, what do you do in the middle of nowhere, with a huge man passed out and bleeding in your car, who is convinced that someone is trying to kill him? Asking for a friend...

I went home, of course. My parents' house and the small town I grew up in was a twenty-minute drive from where I was, and I turned my little car that way and floored the gas. Well, I didn't quite floor it, but I went fast, for me.

My parents were away on a cruise, the first vacation of their lives, and the house was empty. My dad had been the town vet before he'd retired, and I was willing to bet he still had supplies in his small clinic.

Before long, my small, sleepy town came into view. At this time at night, all the houses were shut up tight in the hamlet, and I drove slowly along to the winding drive of my childhood house.

It was rather big, my father had used the annex for his vet clinic, and my mother another side of the house for her tutoring. I parked on the flagstone driveway outside the clinic. Silence fell, broken only by the occasional hoot of an owl outside.

I looked at the man. He had passed out a while back, I hoped from pain, rather than blood loss. I got out of the car and hurried to unlock the clinic doors. Inside smelled a bit musty, but not too terrible. Despite being retired, my father still saw the odd patient, free of charge so he kept the clinic in good shape.

Inside, I snapped on the lights and went to the cupboards in the exam room, looking for supplies. He kept the room well-stocked, and short of a blood transfusion, I should be able to manage something.

He should be in a hospital, my well-meaning, prim, and proper rule-following voice whispered in my head. The voice was constantly with me. I wasn't a rule breaker, I'd leave that to my friend Sofia. It was crazy to be considering trying to patch this guy up at home, alone, and yet, something in his desperate tone had convinced me on a cellular level that it was too dangerous to take him to a hospital. Some intuition told me that if I did, I wouldn't be saving his life, but putting it on the line. As a nurse, I just couldn't willingly do that. Maybe I should call the police? But Maxim Volkov's business was hardly the type you wanted the police involved in. I could speak to Pru, but I wasn't calling her on her wedding night to tell her that I'd picked up a straggler from the wedding, oh, and he'd been shot.

Pulling myself from my circular thoughts, I went outside and opened the passenger door. The man didn't move.

"Excuse me? I can help you, but you'll have to get yourself inside," I said to him, shaking his shoulder. I didn't have a wheelchair here, and there was no way I was lifting such a tall man. "Excuse me, sir?" I tried again, bringing my face close to his, and touching his cheek. His long dark hair hung in strands across his face, and I brushed them back. He had to wake up and get inside, or all this was going to be pointless.

When I touched him, his eyes sprang open, and his hand knocked mine away and fastened around my throat. I cried out in surprise, as the man squeezed my neck, his dark eyes furious for a moment, as it felt like he stared into my soul. I pulled at his hand madly, coughing as my air supply failed for a moment, and then, the pressure was gone. I staggered back from the car, rubbing my neck, as the man stared at me, confused for a moment.

"What are you doing? I'm trying to help you," I demanded. He swallowed and swayed woozily in the seat. He nodded and tried to push himself up.

"Sorry, reflex," he started, and staggered to the side. I went to support his side, and pointed toward the open doorway, spilling light into the dark night. His weight leaned on me, and we started toward the door in a graceless stagger.

"Just get yourself in there," I told him firmly, using my best nurse voice. Nurse voices are magic. They can convince even the most difficult people to shut up and follow directions.

If he fell, there was absolutely nothing I could do about it, and so, we weaved toward an exam bed, while I held my breath and hoped beyond hope that we would make it.

"You are much stronger than you look, Nurse Dani," the man said, as we approached the exam table. His strength failed toward the last few steps, but he managed, collapsing onto the leather exam table with a grunt, and almost rolling right off the other side. Admittedly it wasn't really for people of his size, but it was the best I could do.

"Yeah, well, part of my job is manhandling men like you,"

"Shot?" he offered.

"Trouble," I clarified, and he let out a choked laugh at that.

"You're funny. I like that. I haven't laughed in a long time,"

"Well, to be fair, you don't really look like you've had much to laugh about," I said, tugging him about on the surface, arranging him so he was mostly on the narrow bed, checking his pulse, and taking in his color. He had olive skin, but that looked pale under the clinic lights. His pulse was strong, however, a good sign.

"I'm a firm believer in laughing when your life is going downhill," he muttered. "Close the doors, hide the car… no one can know I'm here," he continued. I paused.

"Hide the car where?" I asked.

"*Dorogiya*, how should I know? This is your house, but don't underestimate them," he muttered. I sighed. I felt half-demented with these crazy warnings heaped on top of the responsibility of caring for someone like this. But, I'd committed to this, I might as well see it through. I grabbed my keys and went outside again, driving the car up the narrow lane to the side of the house, one that was hidden from view.

I went back to the clinic and found my mystery patient passed out again, I stared down at the man who had come so suddenly into my life in such a dramatic fashion. He was wearing a threadbare t-shirt under his hoodie, and I could see the material was wet with blood. I took scissors from a drawer and started to cut. I had to see what I was dealing with.

His torso was bathed in blood, and I snapped on gloves and prepared to clean it. I had to find the sight of the bullet's entry. I washed him, sending rivulets of blood pooling to the floor as I attempted to clean the sorry mess of this stranger's body. It wasn't only the wound I found, but bruising and old scars, a multitude of them. His body had been abused for a long time, and it sickened me to see it. His arms were not only bruised as well but held old scars and marks, a distinctive pattern that told me he had been an intravenous drug user at some point not too long ago.

The bullet had taken him through the shoulder and seemed to have passed right through. It was a blessing, as much more I wouldn't have been able to deal with alone. However, he'd lost blood and was weak. Not just from the blood loss, but the signs of previous beatings. I poked around at the hole cleaning it, grateful that the man had at least passed out and wasn't in pain. The bullet seemed to have missed the subclavian artery, and the brachial plexus, another mercy.

I washed the wound and stitched it carefully closed. It was nothing I didn't do every Saturday night, albeit, we didn't get many bullet wounds in the UK, however, when I'd been young and in Africa, I'd seen a lot of doctors closing a bullet hole. The sight tends to stay with you. I dressed the wound and prepared a shot of antibiotics for possible infection.

CHAPTER FIVE

*K*arim

I woke to the cold, sharp feeling of something piercing my skin. I lashed out at the sensation and heard metal crashing to the floor.

"For god's sake!" An angry female voice cursed at me, and all at once, I remembered. I wasn't in Russia. I was in England. I opened my eyes to find the same woman as before, the slow driver, standing over me with a syringe in her hand. She scowled in my direction, her pretty little bow-shaped mouth pulling into a forbidding look.

"It's a shot for infection unless you'd like to get sepsis," she said forcefully. The words weren't all familiar to me, but I got her meaning well enough. I realized I was holding her slender wrist between my desperate hands like a reed that I could snap accidentally. I let it go. She rubbed at her white skin, marked pink by my touch. Under her strong expression, there was an undercurrent of fear in her blue eyes.

"I'm sorry. I didn't remember where I was," I explained, trying to sit, and hissing with pain.

"Don't move. I've barely finished patching you up. You

can't move yet. You'll rip my stitches." I tried to see down at my own body, but couldn't lift my head enough. I took in the room with its sterile, medical supplies, and even the bed I was sitting on.

"You have your own doctor's office?"

"This is my father's clinic. No one comes here, don't worry," she said.

"He's also a nurse?"

"No, he was a vet," she said primly, starting to tidy the blood-soaked things from the small table beside the bed. I frowned at her. Her father was in the army?

"A vet?" I repeated, wondering if something was lost in translation.

"Yes, an animal doctor," she explained. She pulled a soft-looking blanket over me, and her calm, efficient energy was soothing. I couldn't help a dark laugh from escaping me. Everyone finds their level, after all.

"That's oddly fitting. Will I die?" I wondered.

She shook her head.

"I don't think so, you shouldn't anyway, barring anything terrible happening." She looked down at my body. I could imagine the horror she saw there. I had long ago felt separated from the bag of bones that Igor kept to blackmail Elena with. I was beyond the flesh now, pain, fear... it all appeared as something far from me, but I could read the worry on this woman's face. Dani, she'd said her name was Dani. A man's name in Russia – Daniil, it should have felt wrong to label such beauty so. And she was a beauty, like an angel of mercy, sent to me at the end, my darkest hour, to ease my passing. She had soft reddish-blond hair, the color of wild honey, and blue eyes like a sapphire. I had almost forgotten that such beauty existed in the world. She was studying me closely, a worried frown inching between her large, luminous eyes. She felt my cheek with the back of her hand and stroked my hair back. I didn't know what I looked like anymore. I hadn't done more than glimpsed my face in years. I felt wild and overgrown. A thing of darkness pulled into the light. She eased my hair back, and it felt too intimate for a moment. Her probing gaze looked too deeply inside and saw it all. All the pain and humiliation, all the bargaining and fear.

"You should rest. You're safe here. Rest," her soft words floated to me as I felt my eyelids droop heavily.

❀

*D*ani

So, what did you do to occupy your time when you had an injured fugitive in the other room, you were operating on no sleep, a long day, and the paranoia that either the Russian mob or the police might burst in at any moment?

I locked every door in the place, turned out most of the lights, drew the blinds and curtains, and cleaned up the clinic. It wasn't very comfortable on the exam bed, but I couldn't move him, so I left my mystery patient in the annex, locked it securely. Whether I was locking him in, or others out, I don't know, but if I had any chance of sleeping, it would only be behind a locked door. I went to the main house and poked around in the kitchen. Nothing like a late-night adventure to make me ravenously hungry. True to form, my parent's cupboards were stuffed with canned goods and non-perishables. I heated a tin of tomato soup and ate it staring out the window at the driveway. Everything was quiet in the darkness beyond. Nothing moved. Who was this man, and why was he running away? Who wanted him dead and who had shot him? I had so many questions, but there would be no answers until he woke up, if he did decide to tell me, that was. He didn't seem like the kind who would be pushed into revealing anything he didn't want to.

I sat on the couch and looked at my phone. It was late, very late. Too late to call any friends. I was still staring at the light screen, when I drifted off to sleep, unable to keep my eyes open.

❀

I woke harshly to a banging sound upstairs. I pulled myself up from my graceless sprawl on the couch and shivered in the cool morning air. I was still wearing my glitzy wedding outfit, and my makeup felt dried on. I prized my eyes open and listened for the noise. It came again. Someone was upstairs. Even though my feet were moving, my brain was having a hard time catching up this morning, probably because I was operating on about four hours of sleep. I shuffled upstairs, grabbing a heavy-looking bookend on the way, and hefting it over my shoulder. As I made my way down the hall, the bathroom door at the end opened, and my mystery man stepped out.

I blinked at the sight of him.

He was strong-looking, though thin, his skin stretched tightly over muscle, as though he had starved himself for a good long while. He was tall, at least two heads above me, and he had a dark beard, and long hair, which was hanging damply around his face. I hadn't really had the chance to take him in last night, with everything going on, but this morning, as he walked toward me, with only a towel around his hips, his body still wet from the shower, there was plenty of time.

He was handsome, disturbingly so, I realized, as a hot blush scorched my fair skin.

"How did you get in, the door was locked," I stated flatly.

"There was a key under the mat." His deep voice rumbled in his chest.

"So you just let yourself in?"

"I thought you left it for me?" he reasoned, and his expression was neutral enough, but I had the feeling he might be teasing me. It was less annoying than it should be.

My eyes fell to his shoulder, and my dressing.

"That's supposed to be covered underwater," I heard myself say.

"I didn't want to wake you, you were sleeping so…. " his voice was low and throaty, accented with a deliciously exotic tinge, "-soundly," he finished, somewhat diplomatically, considering there had been nothing sweet or graceful about my exhausted snooze.

"We'll need to change it," I said faintly, as he reached me, smelling like soap and something else warm and peppery. I wanted to step forward and smell him better, but thankfully, retained enough sense to keep my distance. He had stopped just in front of me, and it took every ounce of will not to stare at his bare chest. The bruising called to me, and I wanted to ask him about it, as did the old track marks on his arms. He looked alright this morning, not in withdrawal, and I wondered what his story was. I needed to know. A prickling sense of alarm filled me, as his eyes moved over my face. His look was appreciative, I don't know why, considering my slept-in makeup and clothes, but there was flattery to being looked at like that by a man like him. A man I was alone with, and no one knew about. A sense of unease filled me.

"You saved my life last night," he said suddenly, his deep voice wrapping around me, pulling me in.

"I'm a nurse, that's my job," I heard myself saying. He inclined his head.

"I thank you. I'm Karim," he said. Karim. The name was vaguely familiar, but I couldn't quite place it right now, not with the sight he made, standing before me in all his gorgeous, bad boy glory.

"Dani,"

"Yes, you said," he turned to look around the hallway. There were pictures on the walls of my parents and me. All my childhood, documented for all to see. "Where is this place? Are we in London?"

"No, In Hertfordshire still. About an hour outside London," I told him.

"Does anyone know you are here?" he asked. His question made my radar go off, and I frowned at him. He seemed to immediately sense my worry. "I will not hurt you, Dani. You've saved me, and I owe you a debt," he said. His words should be ridiculous, as sweeping and old-worldly as they were, but somehow, coming from this man, they weren't. Not even a little bit.

"We need to change your dressing, and then you should eat something." I turned away and started to my parent's room. I opened a couple of drawers on my dad's side of the room and pulled some sweat pants and a soft t-shirt out. "Here, you can wear these," I said, turning back to him, only to collide with his chest. He was standing just behind me, and caught me, as the collision almost spun me around. My hand accidentally struck his shoulder, and he winced.

"Sorry! Here, take these, let's go and change the dressing," I prompted, flustered. Karim watched me with his dark eyes, and simply nodded, following after me silently.

He was quiet as I cleaned his shoulder and applied another dressing.

"Where are you from?" I asked. It seemed a harmless enough question.

"Russia," he answered quietly, though that was pretty obvious. "You are English," he stated without question.

"Is it that obvious?" I asked, mostly to pass the time as I cleaned his wound. It had to hurt, but he didn't as much as flinch.

"Yes. You are an English rose, no?" he said. I blinked at him, wondering if he was complimenting me at the oddest time, but his expression was neutral. I shrugged.

"Being English doesn't make me an English Rose. You're a Russian that I met at Maxim Volkov's wedding. Does that mean you're bratva?" I dared to ask, without really thinking it through. His dark eyes came to rest on me, narrowing slightly with assessment.

"If I say yes, will you call the police?" he asked. I thought on it a moment, and let out a long, resigned breath, as I started to tidy up.

"If I was going to, I guess I'd have done it last night," I said. "I'd call Max and Pru first, even if it is their honeymoon or Ivan," I told him and jumped out my skin as a strong hand fastened around my forearm. His grip wasn't tight, but warm and strangely electric. I looked down to meet his stormy gaze.

"No calls to Volkovs. Not yet. I am here for a purpose, and I mean them no harm. I cannot speak to them until it is done," he said quietly. I let him hold my arm, the touching weirdly comforting. This mysterious man was real, this wasn't in my head. He was flesh and bone, even if there was an air about him that seemed otherworldly somehow.

"What purpose?" I asked softly. He merely stared at me, and I knew it would be easier to get answers from a stone, than this man. "You're not going to tell me, are you? Why should I believe you then? Maybe I should call Max and warn him," I said. Why exactly I was goading this stranger, I have no idea. The late-night and madness of the last few hours had broken my brain and my survival instinct, it seemed, but I couldn't ignore the feeling I had in my gut that this man wouldn't hurt me.

"You are close with Max?" he asked. I nodded, unsure if that was a good or bad thing to this man. His intense gaze gentled a fraction, and his thumb rubbed a circle over my skin.

"He just married my best friend," I explained. Karim's mouth quirked into the dark, cynical smile that he seemed to have perfected. "And you? Are you close with Max?" I prompted. I was hoping to learn at least that much. His dark smile turned bitter. Brooding and melancholy, and this guy could pull off that intensity as no one could.

"Not anymore, but once I was," he said cryptically, before pushing himself to stand, careless of the hurt from his stitches. His lithe, sleekly muscled torso flexed under the lights of the clinic and it took every effort not to stare. He held a long-fingered hand out to me, suddenly formal, and I found myself putting my hand in his. He shook it gently, his eyes fixed on me in a way that made my throat dry as a desert and my entire body take notice.

"I am Karim Volkov, his brother."

CHAPTER SIX

 ani

That statement sat in a shocking silence for a moment, as I couldn't quite process the words. A million questions formed in my mind, and I opened my mouth to spit them out like machine-gun fire, just as Karim's finger brushed across my lips, silencing me.

"I know you'll have questions," he said. I nodded, transfixed by the touch of his fingers on my lips and his eyes, staring into me. "I'll answer them, whatever you want, but I have a favor to ask first," he said. I swallowed again, searching for the composure I'd long lost. He dropped his hand. "It's a strange one," he warned.

Ten minutes later, and Karim spread his knees and I stepped in between. We were in the upstairs bathroom, and the clean smell of shaving foam filled the air. I gently gathered his face. His own arm was still wrapped at his side from his shoulder wound, and now, he looked at me trustingly as I picked up my father's razor.

"Are you sure about this?"

"I'm sure. I'd like to see my own face again. It's been a while," he said, as I worked the lather through his beard, softening it, ready to be shaved.

"Well, for a dead man, I guess you're looking pretty good," I muttered. For any man, he's looking good.

"That's a compliment I'm sure not many have gotten," he said, his mouth stretching a little.

"Hey. Be careful. I'm not being held responsible for scarring this pretty face before you even get reacquainted with it," I said breezily. Karim raised an eyebrow at me rakishly.

"Pretty? I'm not sure if that's the description that most men dream of hearing from women like you, but I'll take what I can get."

"Women like me?" I asked, my tone was teasing, but my body felt warm.

"Beautiful, smart, confident women," he clarified. I paused, surprised but flattered by the unexpected compliment. He looked up at me. "What? You must know what a knockout you are?"

"If you expect me to protest modestly, well, you're going to be disappointed. I don't get enough compliments to argue about them. Now, stop moving your mouth, or else your lips are in serious danger of being unuseable," I told him with my best, stern-nurse voice, but he merely smiled.

"Now now, we can't have that. I have plans for these lips," he said.

"Plans!" I retorted, my eyes shooting to his with a mixture of embarrassment and anticipation.

"Plans... I can't remember the last time I ate," he said, and his laugh made it clear that the direction of my lewd thoughts had been fully understood. I sprayed more shaving foam on my hand and smeared it across his full lips, only just starting to be revealed. His eyes continued to watch me with a warm look, as I started to shave him gently. There was a strange kind of intimacy that sprang to life at the closeness of such a personal task. I became aware of everything at that moment. All of it. Like a moment you know you'll remember forever, I saw the soft rise and fall of his bare chest, the pulse in his throat, and the soft look in his strong, dark eyes. I scraped the razor up his chin.

"Has anyone ever done this for you before?" I wondered. He slowly shook his head an inch or two.

"I don't trust easily."

"But you're trusting me."

"You could have already killed me a hundred times over. You saved me. No matter what, I trust you," he said quietly. There was something about those words that made my heart soar. Being trusted by someone who doesn't trust easily felt like a strange kind of honor. "Do you trust me?" he asked. It was a question I had to think about.

"I guess I must, I slept with you so close, alone in this huge house, far from our neighbours. There must be something very trustworthy about you," I said, finishing up the shave and swishing the razor in the sink. "I have good instincts about that sort of thing. I developed them quickly with my job. Who are the patients that are going to cooperate? Who are the ones who are going to run when your back is turned, who are the ones who are going to steal, lie, threaten? When I use my professional instincts on you? Yes, I trust you." For better or for worse, that simple fact had already been decided. "Tell me about Max and you, and why you don't want to call him," I asked. I couldn't hold my curiosity down anymore. Karim swallowed hard, his throat bobbing, and I wondered if he was about to lie to me, but his dark eyes looked earnest.

"We used to be very close, but now, we don't talk. I thought by going to the wedding, we might leave the past behind, but some other issues took over. Things that have nothing to do with Max." I wrinkled my nose as I thought about Karim's answer.

"So, why don't you want to see him?"

"There is something I have to do before I call him. Like, a surprise, I have to plan… I really don't want to ruin it before it's ready." It was clear that there was a lot that Karim was not saying in his answer.

"A surprise? It must be a pretty big surprise that you don't want to call your brother, even after being shot," I remarked but Karim merely shrugged.

"Getting shot to men like Max isn't a big deal." I knew that to be true, however, something didn't sit right with his explanation at all.

"He could help you, with the danger you seem to think we are both in,"

"Once I leave here, you'll no longer be in danger." Karim's voice was reassuring, but his words only made my heart fall. I hadn't realized until that very moment how exciting it had been to be around him. That low-level hum of anticipation and electricity between us, practically strangers and yet, this man, seemed more real to me than anyone else in my life right now.

"And you?"

"I can take care of myself," he said quietly.

"Yeah, getting shot really demonstrates that," I said, and dried my hands on a towel. I turned from Karim, frustrated by the things I felt like he wasn't telling me, even while knowing they weren't my secrets to demand. The feeling of being powerless was always irritating. "Anyway, let's feed you," I said. I'd had all the seeing of Karim without a shirt that my body could endure. He needed to cover up, and I needed to cool down.

"Spoken like my dream woman," Karim teased, clearly

glad to change the subject. I tossed him a smirk as I left the bathroom.

"Spoken like someone who hasn't tasted my cooking," I said sweetly and left the room to the sound of his laughter.

arim

Dani cooked food, all the while watching me over her shoulder. She was curious and I couldn't blame her. Talking her out of calling Max or Ivan straight away had been tricky, but she seemed to let it go for now.

The kitchen of the rambling house was warm and clean. I enjoyed the simple pleasure of sitting in a chair, freshly washed and about to eat food prepared for me by a beautiful, kind, and capable woman. It was more than I'd thought I'd experience again before my vengeance was satisfied, and I left this world with no regrets.

Dani moved with purpose around the farmhouse-style kitchen, her movement's economic and confident. I enjoyed watching her. Of course, she was a stunning woman, and for the first time in longer than I could remember, my body had noticed. I hadn't thought about a woman, nor noticed one, in years. When survival takes up your every thought, attraction isn't something with much room to grow or be noticed. Now, safe for the moment, whole, as much as possible with a gunshot wound, watching the most enticing woman I'd ever seen prepare me a meal, my body was waking up from its long sleep. She knew I was watching her. Her fair skin flushed easily, and now and again, her cornflower eyes would shift to me and skitter away. I had hoped that revealing that Max was my brother would ease her, but she still seemed nervous around me. It weighed on me. I didn't want to frighten her, but I knew what I looked like. I had the aura of a man who had been to hell and back, and there was no hiding that I was a ghoul.

"Do you like pasta?" Dani asked me.

"I'll like whatever you cook me," I told her bluntly. I would probably eat poison if this woman served it to me with a smile.

"You say that now, but I am not known for my cooking, so you might regret it later," she laughed.

"*Nyet*, I won't," I said quietly. She turned her face away, her ears turning pink at the top whenever her eyes met mine. I couldn't stop looking at the elegant bend of her neck, nor the small wisps of hair that had escaped her bun, and now curled around her nape. I wanted to touch them.

"Don't be so sure," she joked again. A little later, she announced it was ready and I rose to bring it to the table. "You should sit down and rest. You've been shot, if you care to remember," she admonished, as I took the heavy plates, and brought them to the table.

"It's not an easy thing to forget," I said, as I sat opposite her. The food smelled delicious, and my stomach let out a hard growl at the scent. "Excuse me, I haven't eaten since-," I trailed off, unable to remember exactly when it had been. A furrow worked its way between Dani's reddish eyebrows as she frowned disapprovingly at me.

"Well, you can't skip meals and hope to recover. You'll need strength to heal," she said firmly.

"Believe it or not, skipping meals isn't always a choice," I said. She flushed at that, her eyes dropping from mine.

"Of course, I didn't mean to imply it was. I'm flustered." Her tone sounded annoyed by her own admission. I raised an eyebrow at her, amused by her expressive face. "I'm flustered by you," she continued. Her words were like a punch to the gut. I allowed myself to look longer at her, the womanly curves and soft-looking skin. Her beautiful face and bow-shaped mouth. My body stiffened, blood rushing places it hadn't in a good long while. I was out of practice when it came to the opposite sex. Hell, I was out of practice at even desiring someone. For so long my life had been about survival, and that was all. Now, for the first time in longer than I could remember, I desired something more than food in my belly, a safe place to sleep and to live another pitiful day. I desired Dani.

"I'm flustered by you too," I said lowly, slaking a dark gaze across the beautiful vision she made sitting opposite me. She reddened.

"That's not what I meant," she muttered.

"It's exactly what I meant," I confessed. She looked away, embarrassed, flattered, perhaps repulsed, it was hard to know which. I steadied my fork in my hand and forced myself to eat slowly. Gorging wouldn't do my starving stomach any good. I ignored my impulses to gobble the food desperately, like that man I had lived a year on the streets as, never knowing when he would eat again. It felt like an act though. I sat at the table, upright on a chair, and held a fork in my hand like a man, a human, and not like the beast I felt inside. I wondered if Dani could see through my man's disguise, at the wild animal beneath. "I apologize. I don't mean to make you uncomfortable, when you have given me care and hospitality," I told her. It had to be disgust in her eyes, and nothing more. Who would feel anything less to be

34

admired by a beast-man like me. "Maybe you could tell me more about yourself. I'd like to know who I'm grateful to."

"There's not much to tell. I'm a nurse, I live near Muswell Hill in London. It's too expensive for me, but I like it. I work a lot."

"I'm sure that's not all you do,"

"Don't be sure. It really is."

"Why are you a nurse then?"

"What do you mean?"

"Well, if all you do is work, that must mean that something in your job is worth dedicating all your time to... why do you love it so much?"

"I don't know. It's gratifying, of course, but it's hard. The hours are anti-social often, and if you're not interested in dating doctors or other medics, you don't meet anyone. It's a tough, dirty, high-pressure environment," she said thoughtfully.

"Is the plot twist that you don't really like it at all?" I wondered. Dani laughed out loud at that, a clear, ringing sound.

"No, I love it, despite all that. I volunteered in Africa, in Tanzania, before starting university. I wasn't qualified to help with the medical work, but I loved to watch the team. They were so busy, so determined, you know. The life there was straightforward and humble. I can't explain it. It was simple, and I liked that,"

"Strong people are always simple." The quote of Tolstoy seemed to fit Dani perfectly. Strong, simple, uncluttered with pretension, and unburdened by ignorance. "You found your purpose," I continued. She nodded and looked wistful a moment.

"I always wanted to go back, but I never found the time and now, I don't know. I worry it's too late,"

"it's never too late to change your life," I said quietly.

Dani's eyes rose to mine. She wasn't fearful of me as she had been before. Now she knew, or at least, believed that I was Max's brother, she was comforted and I was glad.

"Does that include your life?" she asked. My smile turned bittersweet, and I couldn't hold her unwavering blue gaze. I stood up from the table and pushed my chair back. The dishes went to the sink, as I started to wash them, in an awkward, one-handed manoeuvre. Dani watched me in silence before picking up a towel and starting to dry. We worked side by side quietly. It wasn't a conversation that could be continued. Not when I felt that she had her whole life ahead of her, and mine was almost finished. "When will you leave?" she asked me suddenly after we'd finished cleaning up.

"Whenever you want me to," I told her immediately. Everything she had given me was already too much. Her eyes ran down me, lingering on my shoulder.

"I don't have to be at work until Monday. Stay till then, to heal and rest. I know you think we're in danger, but this is literally the most boring, uneventful sleepy town in the world. Nothing bad will happen to us here," she said. I could only hope she was right, but her offer couldn't be turned down. I would never be able to take on Igor and his goons while I was hurt. Every day of rest and peace I could get I had to take. Being around Dani longer was another thing I desperately desired, even as I knew it was wrong. I wasn't the kind of man who could dream of a woman like Dani, even in my wildest, most idyllic years. I'd been born to a life of violence and danger, my birthright had been clear from the start. I could allow myself to be near her, and only that. I still had some idea of honor inside me, after all. I was surprised to find it.

ani

I gave Karim the spare room to sleep in that night and changed his dressing once more before I went to my childhood bedroom to sleep. It was Saturday night. I had to get back to London for work on Monday, and I didn't have a clue what to do about Karim.

The past twenty-four hours had been crazy. I was hiding out with a man who could be a wanted fugitive, Max's brother. I could hardly believe the situation, but I did believe him. Karim. When he looked at me in that special way he had, as though he could see deep down inside, I believed him fully. He wouldn't hurt me, of that I was sure.

The other thing I was sure of that night, as I lay in my childhood room and stared at the shadows of tree branches outside moving in the breeze across the pale moon, was that I was attracted to him. More than attracted. I wanted him. It had been so long that I'd gone on enough consecutive dates with the same man that I'd gotten to know even a little bit about him. Usually, dates consisted of dry small talk about jobs and friends, countries you'd traveled to, and the last Netflix binge you went on. Everything was on the surface, and nothing made it beneath. With Karim, right from the first seconds of knowing each other, he'd been open to me, spilling secrets and blood, terrible trauma, and unimaginable pain all around me. Despite that vulnerability, there was nothing soft nor weak about Karim, the opposite in fact. Knowing some of what he'd overcome made him almost invincible in my eyes. He had a quiet strength and power that I couldn't deny, drew me in. I lay in bed and thought of him next door. His leanly muscled body, and tanned skin. His dark, long hair and wicked smile. My body felt alive at the thought of his bare chest against white sheets.

I got out of bed and opened a window, feeling flushed all over. I felt like a teenager again. My body was warm and pliant at the thought of his. I couldn't remember feeling like this for the longest time, maybe ever.

I had a crush.

I, the straight-talking, no-nonsense nurse who was too busy to date had a crush. It was totally unlike me. I barely had crushes in high school. I wasn't a dreamer, I wasn't a romantic. I was a practical person, and yet, as I returned to bed, I felt an odd yearning in my chest to know how Karim was doing. Did his shoulder pain him in bed? Was he comfortable? Would he come to London with me?

My breasts felt heavy and full beneath my vest, and I indulged myself, sliding my hands down to cup them. The nipples were hard, and I knew why. The man next door was having an effect on my body, without even a touch, nor word of encouragement. I must be mad. I was losing it in my old age. I dropped my hands to my sides. It felt wrong, to be getting off thinking about a man who was clearly going through the hardest time of his life. I tried to will my body to calm, and eventually, I have no idea how long later, drifted off to sleep.

※

I woke to the sound of glass breaking, a soft tinkling that scratched at my consciousness until I sat up in bed, my heart immediately ramping up into a full-blown panic. The room was dark and still. The sound had been faint, as if from far off. I got out of bed quietly and listened. I approached my door and eased it open. The hallway was also still, but there was a soft blossoming of sound coming from below, as though a door or window was open, allowing the night noises inside. I knew this house better than anyone, I'd spent my entire childhood in it. I went down the stairs carefully, avoiding every creak or sound that could give me away. My heart was pounding in my chest, and terrible anxiety filled me. Was this the danger that Karim worried about? Had they found him? Why hadn't I insisted that he called his brother before now? I already knew the answer to that, shameful as it was. I had wanted more time alone with this unusual man… and now, he was in danger again.

I reached the lower hallway and heard the sounds from the garden coming from the direction of the kitchen. There was a glass backdoor in there, as well as numerous windows. I started along toward the room, my bare feet soundless against the wooden floor.

I stepped out across the moonlit tiles and had only gone a few steps when hard, strong arms circled me and pulled me back. I met a wall of strength, my back crashing into some-one's chest, as a hand came up to cover my mouth.

"I'm sorry, it's me," Karim's whisper burned at my temple,

and his whole body was meltingly hot against my scantily clad back. I nodded mutely, and his hand moved from my mouth. He stepped away and approached the window. He looked out, bracing his strong arms on the counter. I couldn't make out much in the darkness, only the white of the dressing on his shoulder. "I thought I heard something outside," he said. I took a step toward him and gasped as a sharp pain pierced my foot. Karim swore in Russian and crossed to me in an instant. He lifted me as if I weighed nothing, and carried me to the kitchen table, and settled me on it. "I should have said, there was broken glass on the floor," he said, lifting my barefoot to inspect it. I looked over at the position, and sure enough, it was just by the dryer.

"It's my fault, I left a glass on the dryer," I admitted. It was something I used to do on a weekly basis as a teen. I swallowed a gasp as his fingers found the splinter of glass, and he carefully pulled it free.

"Does it hurt?" he asked, his brow furrowing.

"Not really," I said. The touch of his fingers, smoothing over the small cut was more than nice enough to offset any pain. He studied me, and I could make out more of his features now, my eyes adjusted to the night. His dark eyes looked black in the darkness, as they suddenly dropped over me, taking me in properly for the first time. I was wearing pajamas, shorts, and a vest, so perfectly modest, and yet, as soon as his eyes trailed over my body, I felt that sturdy cotton disappear. The feelings of desire and longing that I'd fallen asleep with sprang back to life inside me, just as I felt the hunger of his gaze. He looked at me like I was something precious, something rare and special. His skin was warm where his hands still touched my foot. He slid his hands slowly upwards, letting my foot lower. His hands ended on my thigh, no longer holding, now, just resting. I wished they would keep moving upwards. I leaned in, I couldn't help it.

Everything in my body was pulling me to this man, and that sudden, unexpected connection between us.

"Who did you think could be outside?" I asked him, surprised to hear my voice throaty and deep.

"Bad people," Karim murmured distractedly, raising a hand to push a hanging strand of my hair behind my ear.

"And you thought to take them on shirtless, unarmed, with an injury?" I wondered. He nodded slowly. "It doesn't sound like a good plan."

"I couldn't stop to think of a good plan. Because you were inside," he said quietly. "Protect first, plan after," he continued.

"That can't be right. I think something is mixed up with your priorities there," I murmured, as he stepped closer still to me, and lowered his head. My lips parted, and my heart thundered with anticipation.

"I'm sure it's not. I promised not to hurt you, and that includes letting any harm befall you because of me." His breath whispered across my lips.

"Well, I do feel safe with you here," I confessed breathily.

"Yet I am the only reason for you to feel unsafe at all," he reminded me. I tilted my face up to him, and I knew my eyes were sending out the clear signal that if he wanted to kiss me, he could, but he held back. I shivered with the feeling of being so close to something wild and alluring, that you want to press forward and touch it, but fear being burned, like moths dancing around a flame. "Dani, *dorogiya*, I'm going to need you to stop looking at me like that."

"Like what?" my voice was breathy and foreign to my ears.

"Like if I kissed you now, you wouldn't slap me,"

"I wouldn't," I said quietly. My words sat there between us. I felt my body getting increasingly turned on. My top felt scratchy on my skin, and I felt hot all over.

"You should. I've brought you nothing but trouble," he said. A twinge of rejection filled me, at his discouraging words.

"Maybe the truth is that it's you that doesn't want to kiss me," I challenged. I never was able to gracefully admit defeat.

"I've wanted to kiss you from the moment I met you, bleeding out and all."

"So, do it," I heard myself say, a desire straight from my subconscious.

"Do it?" he murmured softly, and I could only nod madly. His lips curled in a smirk, just before he kissed me.

The touch of his lips was hypnotic and startling. A sudden rushing pleasure that tugged at every part of me. He kissed me confidently, parting my lips and sliding his tongue inside, caressing my own in a deeply wicked, wet way. He tilted my head, taking a strong grip on my chin and using the angle to push deeper inside. The slow, erotic slide of that feeling was undoing me. I pulled at his back, bringing him closer, as he devoured me. I could feel that kiss right down to my bones. I sucked on his lower lip, nibbled on it, as he growled lowly in his throat. I felt resistance in him, a barely contained passion that I wanted to break free. I slid my hands down his hard torso, and just inside the waistband of his borrowed sweat pants. Karim muttered a deep gasp and pulled back.

"Dani, I can't. I can't kiss you for even one more second, because if I do... I'll lose control," he admitted quietly. I stayed where I was, my hands grasping greedily into the space where he'd been.

"Maybe I want you to lose control," I told him. He shook his head slowly.

"Believe me, I want to... I want to with you, but I can't. If I lose control, for even a moment, if I look away from my purpose, for even a second... I'll fail, and I can't afford to do that. Most of all, I don't want to lead you on. You're too special for that."

"What do you mean?"

"I'm not planning on sticking around, *dorogiya*. I can't, so I don't want to make you any promises I don't intend to keep."

'Well, thanks for your honesty, I guess. It's pretty gentle-manly of you," I said lightly, hiding the disappointment that stung me. I wanted to kiss Karim, hell, I wanted him to pick me up and take me to bed, consequences be damned. I'd never been so instantly attracted to someone. Ironically, his gentlemanly behavior was only making me want him more.

"You deserve more than a wretch like me," Karim said quietly, and the self-loathing on his face tore at my heart. Before I could argue with that statement, he turned away and looked toward the door. "Now, go back to bed, before I forget how to be a gentleman."

43

CHAPTER NINE

arim

Another meal cooked for me. Another new, best day. Dani smiled at me, as she set the pasta on the table. I looked at it without comment.

"It's the only thing I know how to make," she said after a long moment.

"Fine by me, it just happens to be my new favorite," I told her, digging in. It was lunchtime on Sunday, and I was feeling better by the minute. The kiss last night in the moonlit kitchen filled my mind at every moment I let my guard down. I didn't even try and keep my eyes from Dani now, I watched her unashamedly fascinated by everything about her.

"I have questions," Dani said, as she ate, and pulled her legs up on the chair to sit cross-legged.

"Ok, I will try to answer them, as much as I can," I told her. Dani twirled her fork in her pasta, and then let it rest, cupping her face, and fixing me with her honest blue stare.

"I had heard that Max's brother was dead," she said and narrowed her eyes at me. "Is that you?"

"Yes, I am the dead brother," I confirmed.

"Why does he think you're dead?"

"Because, I did almost die, a year ago. Only dumb luck saved me, and the pity of one of Orlov's men."

"Orlov is the name of your sister's fiancé, isn't it?" Dani asked innocently. Anger welled in me at just his name.

"He is her captor. She has been held by him, in my name, for years." Dani's brow crossed in confusion, and I knew the convoluted story was difficult to follow in parts, as I told it. I took a long drink of cool water, so clean and fresh, even from the tap.

"When Max left for England, I thought I would save both Elena and me from his corruptive influence. I was a student, idealistic, headstrong, and I judged my brother harshly. I started a job, innocent enough, for the Orlov family. They aren't bratva, not officially, but they are obscenely rich. I made a mistake, but once I'd realized it, it was too late. Igor Orlov had convinced Elena that he was a good man. Someone to be trusted," I broke off in a bitter laugh, pain creeping over me as always. The thought of everything my sister had lived through was torture more terrible than any jailor could imagine. "He was far from that, but by the time I'd realized, she'd flown into his golden cage, and he used me, to clip her wings. By threatening both of us with the other's safety, he kept Elena beside him and made her push Maxim away. He had no idea what was happening. He already knew how I judged him, and so, he wasn't surprised when I cut him from my life. Max let me go because he thought I'd be happier that way," I stopped to take a long drink of water, and try and wet my burning throat.

"What did you have to do for Orlov?" Dani wondered.

"Whatever dirty work he didn't want any of his other

men to do. I worried about Max's soul becoming unredeemable, and then became worse than he's ever been."

"I saw your arms," Dani stated, without judgment. I glanced down at my inner arms, already scarred and marked beyond repair.

"Igor keeps his men loyal with fear, and vice. When he started to think I was a flight risk, he started to drug me. I haven't touched it since I escaped," I told her. The hard days after I'd been left for dead returned to me, shivering in alleys in the rain, withdrawal setting my body on fire, and misery like nothing I'd ever known pouring from every pore.

Some of that anguish must have shown on my face, as a sudden, gentle touch to my hand shook me from my dark memories. Dani covered my hand with hers. Her empathy shone from her kind eyes. It was an odd thing, to be looked at so kindly, after the story I'd just told. Unexpected, and unearned.

"That can't have been easy," she said quietly. My mouth pulled into an involuntary grimace at the understatement.

"What was harder was finding the will to survive it. It would have been so much easier to give in then, and die. You must think me very Russian, to have such morbid thoughts," I tried to lighten the heaviness of my words.

"You're right," she said. I blinked at her, surprised by her agreement. "It would have been easier to die. You must be strong to have decided to live, stronger than I can imagine," she said. My throat tightened, an involuntary, startling storm of emotion building inside me. I felt cut open and laid bare before this exceptional woman. All my secrets and darkness, pouring from me in all its ugliness. I found my fingers gripping hers. To be touched felt like a miracle. To be looked at with understanding and empathy... that felt like something I'd never expected to see again. She was looking at me with a tenderness that made my cracked and broken heart feel odd in my chest. I felt seen, for the first time in years.

"Make no mistake, Dani. I'm not a good man, and I am not that strong. The only thing that drove me was the need to save Elena and right the wrong that we have lived."

"But didn't you know! I heard from the security when I was leaving that something happened with her, she left with someone… everyone was talking about it," Dani said, her eyes suddenly brightening. Her excitement to share with me was palpable. This woman. I could fall in love with this woman if I wasn't already there.

"Da, I know this too. I found it out, just before this," I waved vaguely in the direction of my shoulder. Dani nodded, her eyes bright. I suddenly realized that she hadn't let go of my hand. That tendril of connection was so heartening and enjoyable, so real, I couldn't bring myself to pull my hand away first. I hadn't been touched by another in so long, I wasn't only starved for it, but desperate.

"So, that means it's over, right? We can call Max, well, not Max, as he's on his honeymoon, but Ivan, and tell him-,"

"*Nyet*, Dani, no. It wasn't only saving Elena that drove me to survive. It was the knowledge that before I die, I will take Igor Orlov with me," I told her. She jerked at the words, and her hand pulled back from mine. The loss of her touch felt like a blow.

"Do you mean to kill him? Just go to the police," she said quietly, then shook her head. "I should say that, but I can tell by your face, that you don't consider that an option," she finished.

"The probability that he would be punished aside, no. It is no option. For me, imprisonment isn't payment for two lives stolen. I won't rest until he's dead." My tone held no room for negotiation. Dani's soft, kind eyes ran over my face, searching for some kind of compromise there, some sign that

I wasn't just a hell-bent killer, but there was nothing. She could only see the truth of the monster I'd become. She folded her arms across her chest, putting that barrier between us, and I felt her fragile trust and warmth toward me fade.

It was better that she knew now, the type of man I was, than be under any illusion otherwise.

"Why don't you let your brother help you? I'm sure he's experienced enough in dealing with death," Dani said, her voice hard.

"This isn't his death to deal with. It is mine. It is the debt I owe my sister and brother both. No one will take it from me."

Dani pushed her chair out, a loud scrape on the tile floor. She looked upset, and I supposed it made sense. She was a nurse, after all. A caretaker. I was everything she'd hate.

"I'm sorry about what happened to you and your sister, Karim. I can't even imagine. But Elena escaped, she got away. You could go and find her, and be happy. You don't have to waste the rest of your life on revenge."

"My life was already wasted. This is my fate, and nothing can change it, Dani," I told her. She stared at me a long moment, and I raised my eyes and met her challenging stare. I let her see inside me once more, and all the emptiness and devastation within. I finally let the honest truth of myself come out, and Dani looked shocked and horrified by it. "I already died, all you see before you now is a shell, living for one purpose, and one alone. After it is done, so am I. I have no illusions about returning to the land of the living. Worry not. Once it is done, I will pay for it, as I must," I told her. I pushed myself to my feet and we stared at each other.

"If you really mean that, I can't let you stay here anymore. I'm a nurse, I can't live with someone who plans to go out and commit cold-blooded murder. I just can't," she said quietly. I nodded. It was what I'd expected, but it still stung to lose my little ray of sunshine so quickly.

"Then, I'll go now and I vow, you'll never have to see me again. I thank you for saving me, for putting yourself at risk to rescue a stranger, though, you may well be regretting it now," I said. Dani shook her head faintly.

"I'll never feel bad about saving someone's life," she said quietly. She watched me as I headed out of the kitchen. I had little to take with me and I had already lost too much time. I needed to be tracking Orlov down in London and finishing all this. "What do I say to Max? That I met his brother, and never even told him before it was too late? How do I face him?" Dani called to me. Her voice was rough with some emotion that I couldn't bear to consider. To have this woman be sad for me, even for a moment, was more than I deserved.

"We never really met, Dani. I told you, I was already dead long before we met. If you need to tell him anything, simply tell him you met my ghost."

CHAPTER TEN

ani

Ok, so the first few days after Karim left my parent's house were rough. I can't say exactly what kind of spell he put me under, but I thought of him constantly. His dark humor, and self-depreciation, his pain and guilt, only offset by that sudden, and startling sight of his real smile, buried under layers of trauma. I was a mess, and it was totally unlike me. I felt guilty I had sent him away. I should have tried harder to make him change his mind. I felt relieved that he had gone, and I wouldn't fall anymore into an obsession with a man hell-bent on dying. I tensed whenever a dark-haired man was brought into the ER and worried that someday, it might be him, having finally accomplished his goal of revenge at any cost.

I cried a lot and moped around. I never moped about. I was the busy one, the one who never had time to think too much about others, outside my job and family, but Karim had somehow wriggled right under my defenses and now lived in my head, rent-free, and tormented me.

It must be because I knew his secrets. Max would probably kill me to know I had met his brother, who he thought was dead and hadn't told him. I could only hope that wasn't going to be a literal killing. I flip-flopped between thinking I should just call Pru and tell her everything at one moment, and then, respecting Karim's clearly lucid decisions.

I went to my shifts at the hospital, and I went home. I shopped and microwaved dinners before collapsing exhaustedly into bed at night. I tried my best to drive thoughts of Karim and his well-being from my head. If I wasn't worried about his wound and safety, I was worried about his revenge plan. I was a mess, and on Friday night, just before a rare weekend off, I gave up trying to fight it.

I let my co-workers pull me into dinner and drinks, and chased after the oblivion of socialising to give my heart some relief.

"Just take a taxi,"

"I live right around the corner," I insisted later, as my colleagues piled into a taxi sitting at the curb.

"Still, it's late."

"It's fine, I'm not drunk," I told them. They, on the other hand, were most definitely drunk. They waved and got inside, and the black London cab pulled away. I watched it go a moment. I envied their light-hearted laughter and silly tipsy giggles.

I started home, gradually winding my way past streets of pubs and gaggles of people. The weekend was always lively in London, and this one was no exception. I felt like a ghost walking through them. My earlier buzz faded, and I shivered. It was cold and dark, the streets of my small neighborhood were quiet, after the busyness of central, and thoughts of Karim crowded back into my mind. What was wrong with me? I'd known the guy a few days, we'd kissed, and only just.

Why couldn't I get him out of my mind? Even as I knew it was silly, I also perfectly recognized that I would remember that man, and those days together, for the rest of my life.

Behind me, a noise sounded down an alley, crunching glass. I turned to glance back and saw nothing behind me. I walked on, a little faster now. All these maudlin thoughts of Karim and daydreaming, when I should be concentrating on getting home in one piece. London was hardly the safest city in the world. I wrapped my arms around my middle and walked faster. My mind raced ahead to my route. It was all open, and near the road, safe enough, except for one part, where I had to cut through a small close to get to the main street. Nerves sprang to life in my belly at the thought. It was no foreign feeling, this apprehension, and yet, it never got any easier. It was simply part of being a woman, living alone in a big city, or maybe anywhere. Planning ahead, strategizing routes to avoid danger. It was the world we lived in, and it took too much energy to be angry at it right now when I had to stay sharp.

I turned the corner onto the close, feeling the tight space between towering walls crowd in.

I walked quickly and strained my ears for a hint of noise behind me.

There, footsteps.

Footsteps speeding up toward me. I glanced back and stifled a cry as I saw a man in black just behind me, running in my direction. Abandoning any thoughts of looking silly or overreacting, I started to run.

I sprinted up the alleyway, my eyes fixed firmly on the rectangle of main street I could see ahead, moving ever closer. A noise sounded behind me, a gasp and grunt, and then a thump. Fear filling me to the brim, I pushed myself over the last few steps to clear the alleyway and stopped in the middle of the pavement. A few stragglers on their way

52

home from nights out walked around me, giving me strange looks as I stood panting, and staring into the darkness of the shortcut. A shadow moved into the light and I forgot how to breathe for a moment.

Karim looked different, even though it had only been a week. He looked stronger, more vital. He moved with purpose toward me, and put an arm out to steady me, as I stared up at him.

"It's ok, Dani, I'm here," he said quietly. I could only stare numbly up at him until I saw a fine spray of red against his cheek.

"Are you hurt?" I asked immediately. He shook his head.

"It's not mine," he said, and shifted to look back down the dark close. "Come on, I'll take you home."

"The man was following you from the bar you were at," Karim said, as he toweled his face dry. I couldn't stop looking at him, the man I had been thinking about, suddenly here, in my house.

"It seems like he wasn't the only one," I remarked dryly. "Were you following the man, or me?" I wondered aloud.

"You," Karim admitted, and his words made my heart leap into my mouth. "I've been worried since I found out that Igor is checking into every party guest he can. Since enough of them were in Max's world, there isn't much he can do, and a smaller chance that they would have helped me. You are the bride's friend and a nurse… He will look at you closely," Karim said.

"Why?" I demanded as I boiled water for tea. I had to keep busy, or I'd find myself sitting and staring at Karim with my tongue hanging out.

"He wants Elena back, and the only way he can think to do it is to find me first. Without me, he has no leverage."

"And he doesn't think Max will get involved?" I asked. Maxim Volkov owned London, he could crush Orlov without breaking a sweat. Igor's audacity was stunning.

"He's desperate. Having Elena has been the only thing stopping Max from taking everything from his family years ago. It's the only reason he was after my sister in the first place." Karim turned from the window he had been staring out and looked around my flat with curiosity. His eyes drank in the small, neat space, and a soft smile curved his lips. He went to the fridge, where I had my pictures from Tanzania tacked up. He grinned as he looked at them.

"God, you look white in these pictures," he teased me. I knew the one he meant. I was pale and insipid looking, covered in freckles and suncream, with my red hair tied in a knot on my head.

"That must have been the first day. All the others I was red as a lobster," I recalled. Karim laughed, and turned, wincing a moment, before shrugging it off.

"Let me see your shoulder," I said immediately. He thought he could go running around the city, beating people up in dark alleys a week after being shot. He turned to me with a resigned look.

"It's fine,"

"You know that you're not getting out of here without showing me, right?" I asked, crossing my arms over my chest and fixing him with a look.

"Right, my mistake," he muttered, just before taking the hem of his t-shirt, and pulling it up and off his head in one fluid motion. His torso was just as distracting and drool-worthy as ever, and I had to try hard to keep my attention trained on his shoulder. I approached him and pulled the soft bandage off. The skin was pink, and the stitches were still neatly closed. His skin was hot under my hand and I felt my face flush at the sudden proximity.

"Where have you been staying?" I asked softly.

"Here and there. This country is kinder to the homeless than mine," he said quietly. He was looking down at me with his usual smoldering intensity, and I knew I could get lost in that look. I could lap up that attention forever, and never be tired of it.

"You can stay here, tonight at least," I heard myself say.

"Dani, nothing has changed,"

"Yes, it has. You saved me tonight," I said slowly. Sure, it didn't mean anything had fundamentally changed, he was still a man hell-bent on revenge at the expense of his own future, but he had been following me... and he was there when I'd needed him. It was a small change, but it was a sign that Karim Volkov had thought about something other than his vengeance tonight. I wanted to glue my fingers onto that tiny hold and not let go.

"I promised you that I'd make sure you were safe. It's not a promise I intend to break,"

"Then you should stay here, how can you protect me otherwise," I asked. The air between us suddenly felt charged with electricity. As though one wrong move could ignite the air.

"Dani... I can't,"

"Why?"

"Because I'm not the man for you, and if I stay here... I'll want to be," he said quietly. His deep voice filled me with longing as I'd never known. I didn't want this man to die. I didn't want him to waste the rest of his life. I didn't want to lose him.

I pressed myself on my tiptoes and touched my lips to his. He stilled and barely seemed to breathe, as I gently kissed him. I coaxed his lips to move against mine, as I pressed myself closer to his bare chest. I wanted him so badly, he'd taken up residence in my head and my heart over the last week, and there was no escaping this unscathed. If I was going to fall into obsession with Karim Volkov, I was going to fall all in, without regrets. Maybe, just maybe, I could find a way to make him want to live again, in the process.

I let my hand cup his cheek, as my lips pulled at his. He shifted closer and I felt his resolve weakening. Had he missed me, as I'd missed him? My hand fell to his shoulder, and lower, to his chest. I felt the strum of his strong heart beneath my hand. Evidence that this man, unexpected and rare, the man who had turned me inside out within hours of knowing him, was still here and alive... gave me hope.

I had been scared and confused when he left in Hertford-shire. I didn't know my feelings for him were already spreading like a wildfire. Now, after a week of agony and constant lingering imaginings, I realized the truth. It was too late for me. I was already gone on this man. I couldn't let him throw his life away, without giving him something to hold on to.

"I don't care about tomorrow, I just want you, if you want me," I half-whispered to him. His hands came up to grip my arms, and his strong fingers pulled me closer still.

"I've never wanted anyone, like I want you, Dani, I just don't want to disappoint you, when I leave," he said quietly. Leave. He meant to die. Die. I couldn't let that happen. I just couldn't. I kissed him again, and this time his restraint was already stretched too thin. With a tortured groan, he gave into the desire raging between us and swept me into his arms.

"Your shoulder," I gasped, as he urged my legs around his waist and started to walk me through the small flat.

"I couldn't feel pain right now if you shot me again," Karim murmured against my neck, where his mouth was slowly devouring me in hot, open-mouthed kisses that made me tremble. He went unerringly to the bedroom, with my bed clearly visible through the open door. I didn't notice the mess. The half-drawn curtains and empty water glasses on the nightstand were invisible. The rumpled sheets and clothes on the floor disappeared. The world zeroed down to the two of us. Two lonely souls, meeting their mate. The connection between us was the most honest thing I had ever felt. I knew every part of darkness in the heart of the man who held me, every secret, every ugly, unworthy thing, and yet, no one had ever been as beautiful.

Karim dropped onto the bed and laid me beneath him. He kissed me with a searing tenderness that made my heart fly. His hands moved from my hair to my waist and back. Touching me all over, hungry and insatiable, as though I was something to be worshipped, something holy.

I pulled my t-shirt off, and wriggled my panties and skirt down, kicking them off into the darkness beyond the bed, that world that still existed somewhere beyond us. Karim watched me with a look I knew I'd never forget, and then, he covered my mouth with his again, and let his hands cup my breasts, pinching and plucking my nipples until I cried out. He lowered his face to my chest, and took one into his mouth, rubbing across the hard bud of my nipple with his strong tongue. His movements were rough, unrefined. He'd warned me himself that this would make him lose control, and I didn't care. I wanted his passion and wildness. I wanted every part of him.

My hands came up to clutch at his head, and pull his long hair, and he growled against the skin of my belly, as he worked his way lower. I fought the instinctive urge to close my legs, always a little shy about having a man's tongue on me, but Karim gathered my hands by the wrist and held them pinned to my stomach with one hand, as he lowered his face between my legs, and set his tongue against me, his broad shoulders pressing my knees open. He feasted between my legs, his tongue running up and down my slit, dipping inside me, and then up to circle my clit. I rocked my hips against his face as he teased me there, letting my hands go, so I could dig my hands into his hair, and he could stroke me with his fingers. His tongue continued its sweet torture, as he slid a long finger inside me, curling forward to touch me in places that made me cry out. He added another finger and started to push them in and out at a steady dragging pace, as he flicked at my clit with hard confident moves.

I came suddenly, the pleasure rushing over me without warning, and I felt my muscles tense wildly, my whole body contracting, as wetness rushed from me and into his mouth. He sat up after a moment, as I lay in a melted puddle on the covers, and lowered his hand to his belt. He slowly undid it, watching me all the while, and slid his jeans down his hips. His dick slapped up against his belly, and I reached out to touch the head, and he took my wrist and stopped me.

"No. I don't need anything to undo me more than the taste of you." His voice was deep, and his eyes intense, as he moved over me, kicking his jeans the rest of the way off. His body covered mine, and I welcomed the feeling of his weight, pressing me into the mattress. I clung onto him, digging my nails into his back, and pulling him as close as he could be. I wanted to hold onto him and never let go.

I raised my hips and encouraged him inside. I was on the pill, and anyway, I didn't want anything between us. There was a wild feeling of abandonment inside me, that what if this was it, the last chance I might ever have to be with this man. I didn't want anything but him and me. It was irrational, absurd even, but hey, that's where I was at right now. I was tired of fighting it.

He pushed inside me without finesse and I welcomed the

stretch. Karim wasn't some practiced playboy who slept with a different woman every day of the week. He was a man with a death wish, a man who was attempting to cut his earthly bonds, a man who'd lived in darkness and pain for too long. I raised my hips and welcomed him inside my body with everything I had.

He started to move inside me and groaned. He breathed out a long, meditative breath, and leaned his forehead against mine.

"Forgotten how good it feels?" I asked him with a slight smile. I needed to do something to dispel the mad urge to blurt out my feelings to him. It was overwhelming, being held by him, having him inside me.

"It's never felt this good… it's not sex, Dani. It's you," he said, his murmur in my ear making me shiver. He slid in and out of me, lighting me up inside. His dick pressed inside me, fit me, in the most delicious way, and I only wanted to be closer to him. My nails pressed into his back as his pace turned hungry, punishing even, pressing me deeper into the mattress with each thrust, where I could feel his balls slapping my ass. His mouth moved to my ear, where his tongue licked and sucked at my lobe, while his voice whispered across my skin. "You were made to fit me Dani, and I was made to fill you." I shuddered in his arms, holding on now for dear life, from the tidal-wave of pleasure that threatened to suck me under. "Meeting you has been the greatest gift of my life," he said, and brought his lips back to mine, kissing me passionately. Lovingly. It was love, I could feel it, wild and free, rushing between us. Love without reason, or logic. Love without long acquaintance or shared experiences. It was nothing like what I had expected love to feel like. It was nothing I'd ever felt before, and yet, I knew it without a doubt, deep in my soul and heart, I loved this man, and he loved me.

"I love you," I murmured, holding his shoulders tight to me, pressing my heart against his, as his sinuous hips continued their brutal pace. I couldn't hold it inside, I couldn't contain it. "I love you," I muttered again, a chant now, rushing from my lips without restraint.

"And I love you, *dorogiya,* more than you realize," Karim murmured, leaning upon corded forearms to look down at me. His hips changed angles and his dick pressed upwards inside me, rubbing against my g-spot. One of his hands fell to my clit, as he continued to push in and out of me, slower now, deeper, leaving no place untouched. He circled my clit, as I felt my orgasm rushing toward me, and then, I exploded. Waves of euphoria washed over me, as I tightened all around him, and he lowered his body back to mine, cradling my face and kissing me, swallowing my cry of pleasure, my abandon, and love, and found his own release inside me.

CHAPTER ELEVEN

*K*arim

I woke in a mess of limbs and Dani, sleep softened and breath-taking. Soft sunlight was creeping over the white sheets of the bed, and I felt whole in a way I had forgotten existed. I breathed in her smell, and the cotton of the sheets, and flowers on the nightstand. My heart twinged painfully in my chest. I couldn't deny that right now, at this moment, I felt like another man. One whose life hadn't been a night-mare of regret and failure, one who might get to live. I felt healed, in those small moments, before my rage and regret pressed in. I wondered then if Dani was right. Maybe I could change my path and just become this man instead. Let my anger go, and be reborn, as someone who belonged here, in crisp white sheets, with a good, kind woman in my arms.

But my hands weren't clean enough to hold her too long, and my soul was too battered. My darkness would spill out, and build with time, I knew myself too well. For all the time I had dreamed as an idealistic young man of being better than my brother, we were still cut from the same cloth. There would be no true peace and no healing with Igor Orlov alive and well in the world. Whether I lived after long enough to heal... that couldn't be known. I pressed my face into the spill of Dani's red-gold hair on the pillow and breathed in deeply. For the first time, I imagined life after revenge. For the first time, a tendril of hope sprouted in the dry desert of my heart, and I wondered.. what would it be like? To be a man again?

Dani's phone played a cheerful alarm, and she bolted upright in bed.

"I'm up," she said groggily. She made me laugh as she swung her tousled head toward me. "You're really here, it wasn't a dream," she said and gave me a smile I was sure would live in my heart forever. I leaned in and kissed her, a long, lingering kiss that pulled us both back onto the bed. "As much as I want to stay here, I have to get to work," she murmured. I pulled back, disappointed.

"What would happen if you didn't go?" I wondered.

"Hmm, I'm not exactly sure, but I think at least 4 people would die," she said, with mock seriousness.

"Well, in that case, we better get you ready," I laughed. Around Dani, I couldn't stop smiling. It was such an unfamiliar movement that my cheeks felt tired. She got out of bed and shuffled toward the bathroom. "I could always give you a hand in the shower," I pointed out. She turned to look at me, her eyes running over my body. Her gaze was always so frank and appreciative. Dani didn't try and hide her feelings or act coy. She stared at me like I was her favorite thing to look at, and I loved to be looked at by her.

"That's true. I've got ten minutes, I guess if you can make them count," she said, biting her lip and giving me a filthy smile, as I effortlessly pushed myself from the bed and started after her.

"Oh, I'll make them count."

I walked her to the hospital, all the way to the steps. It had been no exaggeration that Igor was after Dani, and now, after last night, he'd know she was the key to finding me. I had to keep her safe, and I couldn't give myself any more time to prepare. I had watched him, made my plans and now, it was time to execute them, and him. Today, Igor Orlov would pay for the time he had taken from Elena and I. He would pay in blood and pain and I would enjoy every moment. Whatever happened after, I couldn't think about it. I couldn't think that this might be the last time I saw Dani, this startling, sudden presence in my life, just when it was ending. Before Dani, I'd never questioned where I was headed. I hadn't cared. Now, I felt torn, and I couldn't allow that to grow. I had to be strong and achieve my goal or die trying. I'd come too far for anything else.

"What are you going to do today?" Dani asked, as she stopped on the steps of the hospital, and turned to look down at me from a few steps up.

"Watch this entrance to make sure no one bothers you," I said. It wasn't exactly true, I wasn't going to be here, but I was going to make sure no one bothered her again.

"Just go home and rest up, I'll call you when I finish," she said. I couldn't answer that, I didn't want to lie to her. I simply pulled her in for a long, lingering kiss. I held her close, and I couldn't stop the whisper in my mind that this was it, this might be the very last time I'd hold this woman in my arms. "Hey? What's up? You look so serious. Are you considering getting a restraining order after that... love confession," she said, cupping my cheek and looking at me

63

with her crystal clear eyes. I raised an eyebrow at that and the way she blushed. God, I loved this woman.

"Why would I do that?"

"Because, it's fast… that's all. We don't really know each other that well yet," she explained.

"I loved you already when I didn't know anything about you, except that you were willing to take a chance to help a hurt stranger, and that you were the slowest driver I'd ever seen," I said. She laughed at that and hit my chest lightly.

"Why are you so serious this morning, then?" she prompted, not letting me change the subject that easily.

"I'm not, I'm just… happy. Happy to have met you, Dani. Meeting you has been the best thing that ever happened to me," I told her truthfully. Meeting her was more than I'd expected from my fate. Her eyes narrowed and she tilted her head to the side.

"You're not going anywhere dangerous, are you? You said you'd stay with me a while… figure things out," she started, and I kissed her again. I couldn't refute her words, but I couldn't stand here and tell her that this might be the last time we met.

"You're officially late, don't let those 4 people die, nurse Dani. Get in there," I said to her, stepping back finally, and looking pointedly at the hospital behind. Her eyes widened a moment and she turned and started up the stairs.

"Shoot! Ok, go on and be mysterious. I'll see you later?" she called, already reaching the top of the stairs. She looked back down a moment, and I gave her a smile and a wave.

"I'll see you," I called, and watched gratefully as she went inside.

I watched the door a while, my heart heavy until I knew it was time to leave. The plans had been laid and there was no time to waste. I walked briskly in the direction of Igor's hotel. Dani's hospital was right in the center of London, and while the center was big, today Igor would be visiting a location not far from me. Not far at all. And today, it would be the last thing he ever did.

ani

"So, what do you think, Dani? Is this the year?" My colleague had asked me this morning, pushing a flyer into my hand. I looked down at it, studying the words. A volunteering program, in Africa. Every year the hospital opened up opportunities to go to field clinics in far-flung locations and every year I let those possibilities pass me by. Meeting Karim had done something to me. I was suddenly questioning my safe, predictable life, more than ever. What was I waiting to live for? When had I become so scared?

Now, I stared out at the street below the hospital. I liked to come up to the roof on my lunch breaks, and today, I saw Karim in every dark-haired man who passed in the street below. My body felt alive from his touch, twinging pleasantly in places I'd forgotten about. I wasn't the type to blurt out confessions of love to every guy I slept with, in fact, last night was a first for me. The first time I'd said that particular phrase to anyone other than friends or family. I'd always thought it would be some grand confession, like in the movies, but in real life, the words had been like hot coals on my tongue, ones I couldn't keep inside. Today, I felt unburdened by making that impulsive and honest confession and my mind was already working to weave myself new dreams. It wasn't just the aftereffects of a night of dreamlike lovemaking. It was more. What would it be like to leave this city, and get on a plane, with Karim? To start a new life in a country that needed us, and leave the past behind. For a moment, the longing for it was so intense, it actually hurt. I rubbed my chest, feeling my breath threatening to shorten. I breathed in and out deeply to stay calm. It wasn't an unusual feeling, this threatening panic of time passing by, and things moving out of reach, but adding Karim's fate into the mix of pressures and worries I usually had was making me a nervous wreck.

I felt like I'd found the man I wanted to spend my life with and he... he wanted to die. Maybe that was unfair. He wanted his revenge more than he wanted to live, that was more accurate. And I wanted to stop him, despite his wishes, that was the ugly truth.

I couldn't let him run face-first into a gun. His life was worth more than that. Yes, I'm a nurse, so I'm naturally inclined to preserve life, but it was more than that. I didn't want the man I loved to die, that was a simple truth. Somehow, in the span of a heartbeat, I'd fallen in love with a ghost, and to deny it would be useless. It had happened. Now, I was facing a choice no one wants to make. In making it, I risked saving Karim but losing him at the same time. My watch alarm buzzed on my wrist, reminding me my break was over, and I stood, feeling the weariness of worry settle like a ten-ton load on my shoulders. But nothing was going to move that pressure until I knew what Karim was going to do, or it was done. I wasn't good at waiting. Every second that passed felt excruciating, and I couldn't quite get the look on his face from this morning out of my head. His kiss had been as thrilling as ever but there had been something more to it. Some sad, melancholy tone. Like a goodbye.

My shift went quickly, as they often did. Something I loved about my job was the way the rush of action and effort stopped me from thinking about my own problems. It gave my brain a rest. I was a whirling dervish of motion for that time, and my mind was taken from Karim and my future anxieties.

I almost made it to. I was ten minutes out from the end of my shift. The afternoon light had faded and a deep purplish twilight had fallen over the London streets beyond the wards. There was a lull in emergencies, and the nurses at the station made small talk about the weekend. For the first time in a long time, I felt excited at the prospect of the week and spending it with someone. The flyer about volunteering crackled in my pocket, and I thought of that secret fantasy often. It had grown alarmingly quickly, from a throwaway suggestion by a colleague, to a vision of Karim and I, sitting side by side in a plane, watching out the window as the African sun began to rise across a distant horizon. A new beginning. A new life, together.

The doors to emergency shot open, and paramedics came in with a trolley. The world slowed like it often does when a new accident comes in, and we have to triage the situation quickly.

But this time, time didn't speed up again.

"Multiple gunshot wounds and blood loss," the paramedic

was calling, as a doctor ran toward us, and I reached the trolley.

Then, I understood. That look on Karim's face this morning, it hadn't just been a flight of fancy, or paranoia. It had been a goodbye, after all.

I gripped the trolley and the rest of the world seemed to fade to numb blankness.

There was so much blood. Red against the white of the trolley. Red against the white of his t-shirt. Red against his pallid complexion. His usually golden skin faded to grey. His eyes were closed, and his dark eyebrows looked like a slash across his waxy face.

"Dani! Dani, are you with me?" Lisa, my co-worker demanded as they started to wheel the trolley carrying Karim Volkov through the accident and emergency department toward surgery. I stared at him passing me by and Lisa had to pry my hands off the metal bars of his bed.

"Dani??"

I stared after them. I wasn't on call for surgery at this time, I couldn't do more than watch the trolley pass through the doors toward the OR. Quiet rushed in, and the world still felt slow and out of sync. My eyes fell to the floor. Red against white. Karim's lifeblood splattered across white tiles. I felt time rushing toward me, catching up for all those slowed moments, and then, I was falling to the ground, and darkness rushed in.

CHAPTER THIRTEEN

So, I'm really not a fainter, in fact, I would go so far as to claim, I've never fainted before. It certainly wasn't the sight of blood, I see it every day, but that day, I realized there is a difference between a stranger's blood, and that of your loved one. I awoke with a cry on my lips in a chair in the nurse's station. Someone had left a bottle of sugary sports drink beside me, and I gulped it quickly down while staring at the board updating the status of the OR. I saw the doctor's name who was currently working to preserve the life of the youngest Volkov brother. Alive still, despite what his family thought. If Karim died today, Max and Elena would never have had the chance to say goodbye. The thought broke my heart.

"Patient in the OR has no ID on him, no phone either," Lisa said, as she bustled into the station.

"How is he?" I couldn't help asking, gripping the table edge as I did. She eyed me curiously.

"In surgery, he's a mess, but hanging on. Are you alright? You went down like a ton of bricks," she remarked, sipping her cold cup of coffee like this was just any day and Karim was just any patient.

"I'm fine," I muttered, sinking back into the chair, and staring unseeing at the table in front of me.

"We should find next of kin though, and try and get someone here for him," Lisa continued.

"I'll do it." My voice sounded far away from me. Clinical and detached.

I pulled my phone from my pocket and unlocked it, unerringly, I went to a familiar number, and my finger hovered over the call button. I had no choice, if Karim died, and his family hadn't known he was here and alive, I'd never forgive myself. If he didn't... I would be breaking my promise not to tell. Could I break the promise I made to the man I loved, was that really love? What if I called Max and Karim died, and I had broken the only promise I'd ever made him. The thoughts whirled in my head, a messy, heartbroken storm of pain and indecision.

What was the most loving thing to do in this case? If Karim survived, his brother would never allow him to put himself in harm's way again. He would eliminate Igor himself, with all the might of his bratva, and Karim would live.

Was it selfish to want Karim to live, even if it meant his plans for revenge were unfulfilled? Just because he survived, it didn't mean that he would ever forgive me for that. But I would rather he never forgave me, and that's how I knew it really was love, at that moment.

I barely hesitated, as I pushed the call button.

Let him hate me, if he's alive, it didn't matter. That was love, for me, in the end.

"Pru? I have to speak to you, and you need to get Max too."

CHAPTER FOURTEEN

*K*arim

My name is Karim Volkov, and for the second time in a year, I died and came back to life.

I awoke to a haze of pain, one of the only ways I knew I was indeed still alive and hadn't passed. The other reason I knew I was alive, was because there was a hand holding mine that should I have died, I'd never had been able to see again. An angel, sleeping by my side.

Dani was sitting in a chair alongside my bed, my hand in hers. As I properly woke, the machines on either side of me started to beep madly. Dani sat up suddenly, that same startled awakeness that reminded me of how she woke in the morning. Always alert, a caregiver, healer, a medic. Someone who had dedicated their lives to a higher purpose.

"Karim, don't try and move," she croaked quietly. The doors to the room opened, and another nurse came in, followed by a doctor.

"Good morning, Mr. Volkov. You gave us quite the scare,"

the doctor said warmly. Her name badge read Dr. Whitely. I tried to answer her, but my mouth was too dry.

"Here," Dani said, immediately reaching for a cup with a straw. Slowly, my brain caught up with the Doctor's words. *Mr. Volkov?* What had Dani told everyone? The truth?

"Now, I just need to do some checks, but generally you seem to be recovering very well, and regaining strength quickly." The doctor moved around me, as Dani hovered. Her eyes were red, tearstained and they tortured me. I didn't want this woman to cry ever, and especially not over me. "Very good, Mr. Volkov." The doctor continued, but the words washed over me in a wave of exhaustion. I turned my head to look at Dani, who was staring at me with those tortured eyes. The room behind her looked private, expensive, and I was alone, for which I was grateful. I reached out a clumsy hand toward her, but couldn't quite manage it, and fell back into the darkness of sleep.

The next time I woke, it was night-time. Dani was sleeping in a chair, in her nurse's uniform. I hoped that I wasn't on the list of patients she had to care for, it seemed too cruel a task, to make her clean up the mess I'd made of my body.

"Karim?" A voice spoke, deep and full of wonder. It wasn't Dani, she hadn't moved. I slowly turned my head to face the other way and saw a man standing at the window. His tall, broad silhouette was one I'd recognise anywhere. A man who I knew just from the sound of his soft breath in the room.

"Max?" I managed to force it out. Emotions collided in my broken chest at the sight of my older brother. The man

I'd judged and pushed away, first because of my misguided ideals and later, to keep Elena safe.

"Karim??" Another voice, this one soft and feminine. A voice that in my darkest moments, I'd never thought I'd hear again. Elena.

She rushed toward me, stopping just short of grabbing me up, and I knew then that I must make a sorry sight. Her eyes filled with tears, spilling down her face, and I felt wetness on my own cheeks. Max came up behind her, staring at me with that unfathomable look. He laid a hand on my shoulder.

"Hey, long time, no see," I joked with them in Russian. I never did know how to be serious. Elena let out a cry, and I knew she wanted to hit me, but Max merely smiled, and lightly squeezed my shoulder.

"Karim, brother. I still don't know if this is real, or not,"

"It's too painful not to be real," I said, gasping as I tried to sit further up. Dani woke at the sound of our voices. She jerked awake again and rubbed her eyes, before taking in the scene before her. Her eyes softened at the sight of my brother and sister standing over me, but then dropped to me. I saw guilt in that look. It had to have been her that called them and spilled my secrets. I saw how burdened she was by that.

"Igor..." I started, the most pressing worry taking over my mind. Nothing had gone like it was supposed to, of course not, for nothing in my life had.

"Escaped. He arrived in Moscow two days ago," Max said. The words fell like stones through me. All that, all the pain and suffering and planning, and I hadn't managed to end the one person it had all been for. I shook my head and closed my eyes. I couldn't stand the thought that the man was alive somewhere. "I will take care of him, now, Karim. You have done enough, let me see to it, for both of your sakes," Max said, looking at myself and Elena. I felt my head shake.

"No, I have to do it, I have to be there," I started. It was exactly as I'd known it would be, and my heart rebelled.

"Karim, you're hurt, you can't go anywhere," Dani started, and stopped as I looked at her with all the frustration and disappointment I felt. It wasn't fair, of course, to put all that on her, but at that moment, hurt, returned from the dead, having failed once more, I couldn't help it.

"I need to speak to my family alone," I told her. Dani flinched from my tone, as though I'd physically struck her. She stared at me with her clear eyes, and her expression gradually turned resigned. She nodded, and pulled herself together, folding her elegant arms over her chest, and nodded to Max and Elena, before leaving without a word. I immediately regretted my harshness.

"You shouldn't be hard on her, Karim. She thought you might die, and we'd never had even known you were alive," Elena said, giving me a resentful look.

"I wasn't alive… until I kill Igor Orlov, I am not alive," I told her gently. She shook her head and turned away, her expression told me I was the most annoying and bull-headed person she'd ever met. She was no doubt right. Max though, I could tell in his look that he could understand a little of what I felt.

"I can't allow you to be hurt again. What matters is Orlov dying, not who does it," Max said quietly, and his tone sounded like a command. He was a man used to commanding men and expected obedience.

"This is why I didn't tell you, obviously. Because to you, Elena and I are still little kids you have to feed and protect when in reality, we're all grown up." I trailed off as exhaustion hit me again. I couldn't keep up the conversation for more than ten minutes.

"Sleep again now. We have time to talk about all of this," Max said, nodding to Elena. "Would you like me to get Dani?" Elena asked, clearly already seeing the relationship between us was something more than just friends. I shook my head, the tiredness dragging me down.

"No, I just want to be alone," I told her, and they left me quietly. My heart felt odd in my chest. I was alive, it was more than I'd expected, but Orlov was also alive, which was less than I'd hoped. I was reunited with my family, but the cost of that was to give up my revenge. I loved Dani, but she had gone against my wishes when I'd been unable to speak for myself. I had lived the last years under Orlov's cruel control and the scars of that still marked me. I couldn't get a grip on my thoughts, dark and writhing as they were. I lay back and once more, let my tiredness pull me under.

CHAPTER FIFTEEN

ani

The week after Karim woke up passed slowly. I went to see him, but he was often with his family, and I felt like an outsider. We were never alone. I didn't know how he was feeling about me, or any of it. Whatever had happened with Orlov, both of them had survived. I didn't know how to feel about any of it anymore, but I missed him. I missed the Karim with a twinkle in his eye, the one that laughed and teased me, but held me close and kissed me as if I mattered.

A morning about two weeks after the accident, I went up to Karim's room. He was staying in the executive suite of the hospital, which had to be costing Max a pretty penny, not like he couldn't afford it. Security stood outside the door and one familiar face. Ivan's granite visage cracked into a smile at the sight of me.

"Dani, you are always working, it is too much," he said, as he always did, kissing me on the cheek as a greeting. Sofia's huge, gruff husband was one of my favorite people.

"Look who is talking," I teased him. I stared at the small

window beside the door. "How is he today?" I asked. Ivan tutted.

"You should ask him yourself," he said quietly. He repeated this instruction at least three times a day, because, crazy as it was... I hadn't actually been to see Karim alone since before the night he woke and spoke to Max and Elena. I was too afraid that he would blame me, hate me. I was too afraid of finally finding out that in loving Karim, I had lost him. The knowledge that he hadn't asked for me at all, also kept me away. I shook my head lightly.

"I don't have time to stop, I just wanted to check in with you," I said, taking the coward's way out. Ivan looked completely unconvinced by my words.

"You will have to see him one day," he said.

"Not if he doesn't want to see me, I don't,"

"What do you want, Dani?" Ivan questioned. I thought about it a moment.

"I don't know, honestly. I don't even know," I admitted. Ivan considered my answer and then seemed to make his mind up about something.

"You should know that Max will wait until Karim is well enough to travel to Russia. He understands his need for vengeance. We will go, together, the Volkov Bratva, and end this, once and for all," Ivan said quietly. Dread swept over me, sending my skin up into gooseflesh.

"He almost died, and Max plans to let him have another go."

"He will be safe with us. I will not let him get hurt,"

"You can't guarantee that, and what about you and Max?"

"This is the world we live in Dani, Sofia, and Pru both know that. They have made their peace with it. We can only be the men we are... and this is who we are, Karim as well."

"Life really is worthless to you, isn't it? I guess that's what happens when you deal in death and darkness," I heard myself say, anger and fear making me brittle as if I could just snap in half. I clenched my hands into fists. But I couldn't contain the worry, and Ivan wasn't the one I was angry at. I whirled toward the door to the suite and went inside. Karim was sitting up in bed, and looking so much better. His color was back to that rich caramel and his dark eyes were wide and clear. He looked surprised but not unpleasantly so to see me.

"Dani-," he started, as I marched toward the bed.

"Are you really going to go to Russia and get into some kind of shoot-out, dangerous war to kill Igor? You really value your life so little?" I demanded. Tears were threatening to pour from my eyes, but my anger, spikey and hot, fuelled me.

"I have no choice, *dorogiya*."

"You always have a choice," I insisted. Karim shook his head, and took his dark gaze from me, focusing instead on the window.

"No, I don't, but I don't expect you to understand. We are from different worlds, Dani. You will never understand, and I won't ask you to," he turned back to me, and there was resignation in his eyes. This was it, I could feel it in my bones. The last time I'd see this man. "I don't expect it from you," he finished quietly.

"You said you cared about me, was that just a lie then?"

"No, I do care about you, more than care... you made me want to live again Dani, and I thank you for it. After, when it's finished, I'll return and -,"

"What? We can pick up where we left off, as long as you don't die, of course. Is that caring about someone to you?" I demanded hotly. Karim just watched me, as hot, angry tears finally broke free and streaked down my face. "That isn't caring about someone. That's your vendetta still being more important than living... and I can't wait around and see it.

81

Good luck," I said quickly. I had to get out of the room before I fell apart completely. What a torture it was to love someone who wouldn't let the past go, who wouldn't stop putting themselves into vital danger. I couldn't cope with it. I felt like my heart couldn't be more broken than it was at that moment.

I didn't stop to say goodbye to Ivan, I couldn't look at one more person who understood Karim's crazy death wish. I stormed off the executive floor and down in the lift. I felt sick and overwhelmed and heartbroken, and one thing was clearer than anything else. I couldn't go on like this. I couldn't sit at home, and work my shifts at the hospital and just wait and see if Karim would survive or not. I just couldn't. I had to take responsibility for my own life, and there was no point waiting. Life, precious and short, was passing me by. Not anymore, I thought determinedly, fishing my well-worn flyer out my pocket.

CHAPTER SIXTEEN

*K*arim

The loss of Dani was harder than the gunshots and lasted for longer. I was pretty sure her absence wasn't something I was going to recover from, and yet, I was still resolved to finish my plans. With Max's men with me, I could do it. I would make Igor answer for everything he had done to all of us, and then, I would come back, and see what I could salvage with the woman I loved. Because I did love her, even after everything that had happened to me, my heart was the fastest to heal, and it had started the night I met Dani. I'd loved her from first glance, my beacon in the darkness, and I would dedicate my life to making it up to her, somehow, in some way. If I was alive, I could find a way.

I could see it now, life after my many deaths. This strange and foreign hope for something more was the sole responsibility of Dani. Without her, I still wouldn't care if I lived or died.

The day I was discharged from the hospital, I had to fight

the urge to walk the halls looking for Dani. But she didn't want to see me, I reminded myself continuously. So I left, driven back to Max's hulking mansion in an old, respectable part of London. We made our plans, and Max soothed everything over for me. The shooting, my passport, and papers, or lack thereof. There was no one that the Volkov bratva couldn't influence, and before long, my brother had once again provided for me, this time, a free and legal life in this new country. Now, all that was left was to cut the ties with the past and live. To cut the ties with the past, I needed Igor dead. To live again, I needed Dani. The two didn't seem to go together. In the end, I realized, it was a matter of which was more important. The past, or the future.

"Are you sure this is what you want?" Max asked me one night. I was on my way to being fully healed, though physically I still had to rebuild strength. Day in and out, I thought of the things I'd lost, and my plans for revenge. Strangely, thoughts of Igor Orlov faded, and memories of Dani took over. I thought about her near constantly. My light, in the dark.

"Of course, it's all I have left, my vengeance," I told my brother. He smiled, but it was without humor. It was an expression he had worn often lately, and nothing like the look of happiness and contentment he wore around his wife. I worried him.

"Elena would be upset to hear that. She has left thoughts like that to me. She's been through enough," he said. I shook my head.

"I can't let him get away with it. He needs to know it's me who delivers the final blow,"

Max looked contemplative a second, before turning in his chair and taking a book from his personal library behind him.

"'Respect was invented to cover the empty place where

love should be' - Tolstoy. You told me that line, and I remembered it well these past years. It helped me to see how I was chasing the wrong things in my life. Here is one that comes to mind for you," he said, and passed me over the book. A thick Victor Hugo tome. Les Miserable. "'It is nothing to die. It is frightful not to live'" Max said slowly. The words were too uncomfortable to hear. Too close to the bone. "Sometimes dying isn't the hardest thing to do, that is something to think on, brother."

CHAPTER SEVENTEEN

ne month later

Dani

The sun in Tanzania was as blistering as I remembered it to be, but thankfully for me, as a nurse, I was able to hide inside the medical tents for most of the day, treating patients. I gave vaccines, ran classes for locals on first aid, and treatments for common ailments. Every day, I worked myself to the bone, and slowly, my heart began to heal. I talked with the locals, children full of sunshine and enthusiasm, mothers full of advice and gossip, and fathers full of jokes and stories. I ate and slept. I worked. I walked the small mud-hut village and stared out at the sun rising and sinking into the horizon each day. I tried to turn my thoughts away from my ghost, the man I loved, a world away. Here, there was life. People choosing to live with everything they had, and it filled my heart with gratitude. We were working hard on getting a well put into the town, as the nearest water supply was miles away. The journey there and back took too many villagers an entire day and cost the children school time.

The day that volunteers showed up to put one in was one of the happiest days of my life. I rose early and headed out to the village square. The trucks were already there, unloading supplies.

"Oh, god, I can't wait for this," Lisa, my colleague who'd ended up coming with me on a whim, said from beside me. I watched the blue T-shirted men and women from the trucks carrying their heavy equipment. It was very early so the day was still quite cool, but later, it would be blisteringly hot under the sun. "You know, I heard it was a private donation that got us this well. We were way down the list, despite the locals needing it so badly," she was saying.

"A private donation?" I repeated. I wondered who'd have the type of money to manage it, but it was heartening to know there were such generous people in the world. "I'm heading over to the clinic," I told Lisa, before turning away.

I walked through the small village, to the medi cubes set up at one end. They were small inside, so we had made large outside tented areas to spread the shade and sanitary conditions as well as we could.

I stepped inside and went directly to sanitize my hands when a scuffling sound came from deeper inside the tent. I turned to look. We'd had a couple of problems with supplies being stolen and sold on, but I'd thought we'd stamped it out. The gauzy white tent roof blew gently, as I struggled to see. A figure was standing beside an exam bed.

"Is there a nurse available?" A deep, strong voice called out. My heart jumped right into my mouth. "I'm in need of aid... I was hoping someone here could help me," the man continued. I felt my feet walking in the direction of the voice. The one I heard in my dreams night in and night out.

"I'm a nurse," I said faintly, as I pushed past the last, overhanging material, and I saw him.

Karim Volkov. In the flesh. Here, whole and alive and in Tanzania now, apparently. A private donation. I certainly knew one family who could afford it. He turned to look at me, a familiar grin playing around his lips.

"That's right. You are. You can even stitch men up in a vet's office," he said, taking a step toward me. He was wearing a volunteer t-shirt, the very same one as the volunteers who were digging the well wore. It was pulled tightly over his strong chest. He looked vital and healthy, for the first time since I'd met him, there were no wounds, or scars, at least visible on the outside.

"What's wrong, are you hurt?" I found myself saying, my eyes trailing over him, looking for hurt. Karim nodded, with a solemn look in his eyes.

"I am hurt. I'm in pain, and nothing makes it go away," he said quietly. I could only stand there as he approached. My blood was roaring in my ears and I felt like I was watching him approach me from somewhere far beyond my body.

"Did it happen in Russia? Were you hurt again?" I asked. He shook his head.

"No, I wasn't hurt there. I didn't go," he said quietly. My eyes shot to his, narrowing in disbelief.

"You didn't go?"

"No. I let Maxim's men who are based there finish the job. There wasn't much left to finish anyway, and I decided I didn't need to see it or risk Ivan and Max," he said. I couldn't quite process his words and what they might mean.

"How are you hurt then?" I asked, as my brain scrambled to catch up with events. He touched me then, sending heat and other things I couldn't quite name through me. He took my hand, and lifted it to his chest, right over his heart.

"Here. I'm hurt here, and it won't go away, as long as I'm without you," he said quietly, stepping closer to me, and bringing his hands up to hold my shoulders.

'Why didn't you go?' I asked.

"Because I realized that life isn't really that bad… I mean, there might be something to live for after all. Someone. And I didn't want to risk the chance of never seeing her again."

Tears dripped unbidden down my cheeks. He reached out to brush them away. "I love you, Dani. I love you, and I don't want to be parted from you again. Where you go, I'll go. Let's do something good with our lives, together," he said quietly. I let out an incredulous laugh at his words. Words I had dreamed the like of, but never thought I'd really hear.

"I can't understand, you were so certain…"

"Yeah, but it was misguided. There was a choice to make, and I was confused for a moment, but then it became clear. I choose you, Dani. I'll choose you, every single time. You brought me back to life… and I never want to be parted from you again. If you'll have me," he said finally. I choked back my tears as I jumped into his arms. I pressed my body against his, alive and whole and here.

"Yes, I'll have you. I'll have you, and no one better try and take you from me," I said fiercely as I pulled his lips down toward mine. Karim's grin curved wider.

"So, you'll marry me then?" he asked. Joy exploded in my chest as I laughed and nodded,

"Yes, I'll marry you,"

"You'll be my family?"

"Yes, I'll be your family," I breathed, as he finally kissed me and pulled me close. Close enough to feel his heartbeat.

"Let's do this then, nurse Dani," Karim said, as he finally pulled back when my body was warm and soft, a melted puddle of love and desire in his arms.

"Do this?" I wondered.

"Live. Let's live... I want to, if it's with you," he said solemnly. I held him close, no longer a ghost in my arms.

"Oh, it'll be with me. Just try getting rid of me now."

EPILOGUE

*D*ani

The night drew in just as we got settled in my tent. Kamir wouldn't be leaving with the other volunteers tomorrow. He was staying with me. Forever, apparently, at least that's what the ring would infer.

Where last night the small, cramped space felt like a nightmare of cramped mosquito nets and dim headlamp reading, tonight felt completely different. We crawled into the small camp bed, and I crossed my fingers it would take both our weight. I held my hand up in the dim light and admired my ring.

"Are we really engaged?" I checked again, for the hundredth time.

"We are really engaged," he confirmed, as he shifted us so that I was sitting astride him, and turned his attention to working my t-shirt upwards.

"When will we get married?" I wondered.

"Tomorrow, if you want," he said quietly. I grinned down at him, delighted.

"Really? Here?" I asked.

"Why not here? So, I don't know the process… but I want to be married to you," he said, pulling my t-shirt over my head, and turning his attention to my bra next.

"Marriage. It's so final."

"It is, that's why I want to lock you down, as soon as I can,"

"Well, I did get an offer the other day for my hand for five cows… so you better make good on this promise or lose me forever," I said, only half-joking. Karim's face sobered a little, his eyes tracing up to mine.

"Almost losing you once was enough. I never want to be separated from you again. Nothing is worth that," he said. His eyes dropped back to my bra, and he ran his hands down my chest, and found my nipples, teasing them through the lace.

"Hmm, and they say people can't change. I beg to differ," I murmured. He laughed, low and throaty and sexy.

"I haven't really changed, Dani. You made me remember the person I used to be. I never wanted Max's life, I never wanted that kind of life… I wanted a simple, good life, and fate mocked that desire," his hand slid inside the cup of my bra, and palmed my breast, making me wriggle in his lap.

"What did you say again? 'Strong people are always simple'" I echoed his Tolstoy quote. He nodded, while his thumb strummed at me, making me wet and wanting. "So, what do we do now?"

"Now… we live." Karim's voice, finally full of hope and free of darkness wound around me, comforted me, reassured me, lifted me up. "Let's just live… good, simple lives, together."

"Sounds like a plan. "

The End

I hope you enjoyed reading about the Volkov family!

Look out for my Bad Boy Bratva bundle when it comes out, for extended epilogues on all the couples.

Interested in Maxim Volkov's story, you can read about it here
His Dark Desire

ABOUT THE AUTHOR

Gia Bailey loves to write steamy, sweet, short romances to keep her warm during the cold Scottish nights

She loves writing possessive, obsessive alpha males, who go OTT for the women they fall for
Join the mailing list here
Get a ebook gift here xoxo

Stolen by the Billionaire

Claimed by the Billionaire

Printed in Great Britain
by Amazon